WI1 ✓ W9-ASI-854

9/21

Praise for

ankham Thammavongsa's

How to Pronounce Knife

Winner of the Scotiabank Giller Prize

Finalist for the National Book Critics Circle Award for Fiction

Finalist for the PEN Open Book Award

Longlisted for the Believer Book Award

Honor Title for the Asian/Pacific American Award for Literature

"The title story of poet Thammavongsa's debut fiction collection centers on a young girl who can't pronounce a difficult word, so she asks her father for help. Her question is simple—but his answer provides unforeseen ramifications for both child and parent. The interaction is indicative of the deceptively devastating power of these strange but biting stories, which are focused on Lao immigrants living in an unnamed North American city. Their narratives also share a harsh reality of their circumstances: understanding the boundaries of language and how those restraints relate to privilege."

—Annabel Gutterman, *Time*

"An impressive debut…Thammavongsa's spare, rigorous stories are preoccupied with themes of alienation and dislocation, her characters burdened by the sense of existing unseen...Her gift for the gently absurd means the stories never feel dour or predictable, even when their outcomes are by some measure bleak...It is when the characters' sense of alienation follows them home, into the private space of the family, that Thammavongsa's stories most wrench the heart."

—Sarah Resnick, *New York Times Book Review*

"In Thammavongsa's work, refugees don't have to be just tragic or sad but can be imbued with humor, complexity, and the unexpected. Most importantly, Thammavongsa doesn't write for a white audience. She writes, tenderly and profoundly, for her characters...The power of *How to Pronounce Knife* lies in seeing the unseen. I know that firsthand—as the daughter of refugees, I'm able to finally see myself in stories."   —Angela So, *Electric Literature*

"Fourteen piercing sketches illuminate the workaday routines and the interior lives of Laotian refugees. Characters who undertake 'the grunt work of the world,' laboring in poultry plants, hog farms, and nail salons, also harbor vivid fantasies...brief glimpses of freedom in otherwise impenetrable places."   — *The New Yorker*

"These poignant and deceptively quiet stories are powerhouses of feeling and depth; *How to Pronounce Knife* is an artful blend of simplicity and sophistication."

—Mary Gaitskill, author of *Veronica* and *Somebody with a Little Hammer*

"Brings to life characters that might otherwise not figure on the literary radar, from a failed boxer turned manicurist to a young woman working at a chicken-processing plant and a mother-daughter worm-harvesting team, with enough panache to keep the reader gripped throughout."

—Emma Specter, *Vogue*

"Reading Souvankham Thammavongsa's *How to Pronounce Knife* is like finding, at last, a part of you that you had lost and had been searching for all this time…This is a book full of powerful resilience, great journeys, and above all else: fierce, heart-wrenching love."

—Paul Yoon, author of *Run Me to Earth*

"I love these stories. There's some fierce and steady activity in all of the sentences—something that makes them live, and makes them shift a little in meaning when you look at them again and they look back at you (or look beyond you)."

—Helen Oyeyemi, author of
What Is Not Yours Is Not Yours

"Souvankham Thammavongsa writes with deep precision and quiet, cool, emotionally devastating poise. There is not a moment off in these stories."

—Sheila Heti, author of *Motherhood*

"In sparse prose braced with disarming humor, Thammavongsa offers glimpses into the daily lives of immigrants and refugees in a nameless city, illuminating the desires, disappointments, and triumphs of those who so often go unseen... Though short enough to read in one sitting, this collection feels vast in its scope, offering ample room to wander."

—Cornelia Channing, *The Paris Review*

"Thammavongsa isn't just gifted at exploring the dynamics of families adjusting to new lives, she's also an immensely talented writer. *How to Pronounce Knife* is a wonderful fiction debut that proves to be a perfect showcase for Thammavongsa's skill with language and her abundant compassion. It's also a reminder of our shared humanity at a time when we need it most."

—Michael Schaub, *Minneapolis Star Tribune*

"Thammavongsa's careful dissection of everyday moments of racism, classism, and sexism exposes how power and privilege drive success, how work shapes the immigrant identity, and how erasure and invisibility lead to isolation." —Jenny Bhatt, *Washington Post*

"Thammavongsa has shown herself to be a master of controlled intimacy, eschewing preciousness in favor of a clear-eyed humanity. She maintains this unsentimental beauty in her debut collection of short stories, *How to Pronounce Knife*... It is tender, funny, and even sexy at times... Thammavongsa has made English speak to us in her own language." —Nay Saysourinho, *Ploughshares*

"Tinged with melancholy, anger, and a healthy dose of dark humor, all of these stories exhibit a fierce pride in what one can accomplish. After leaving everything behind and dealing with a country that does not cater to you, one can still celebrate the resilience of the human spirit by merely surviving."　　　　　—Hanh Nguyen, *Salon*

"*How to Pronounce Knife* is a masterful collection, written with so much veracity, you'll swear every word is true. Thammavongsa offers sharp sensory details, piercing imagery, endings that will punch you in the gut and leave you yearning for more."
　　　　　—Sharon Bala, author of *The Boat People*

"Every once in a while you come across a book with writing so breathtaking that you take note of the author so you can read everything they ever write in the future. *How to Pronounce Knife* is one of those books. The author's debut collection weaves vivid tales about immigrants in a nameless English-speaking city."
　　　　　—*Elle Canada*

"In *How to Pronounce Knife*, Thammavongsa plumbs the depths and superficialities of what it means to be human. She's at ease in the dark. With authority, her fiction asks: How do we survive? What does it mean to endure?"
　　　　　—Zach Davidson, *Bomb*

Books by Souvankham Thammavongsa

Fiction
How to Pronounce Knife (2020)

Poetry
Small Arguments (2003)
Found (2007)
Light (2013)
Cluster (2019)

HOW TO PRONOUNCE KNIFE

Stories

SOUVANKHAM THAMMAVONGSA

Back Bay Books
Little, Brown and Company
New York   Boston   London

Copyright © 2020 by Souvankham Thammavongsa

Hachette Book Group supports the right to free expression and the value of copyright. The purpose of copyright is to encourage writers and artists to produce the creative works that enrich our culture.

The scanning, uploading, and distribution of this book without permission is a theft of the author's intellectual property. If you would like permission to use material from the book (other than for review purposes), please contact permissions@hbgusa.com. Thank you for your support of the author's rights.

Back Bay Books / Little, Brown and Company
Hachette Book Group
1290 Avenue of the Americas, New York, NY 10104
littlebrown.com

Originally published in hardcover by Little, Brown and Company, April 2020
First Back Bay trade paperback edition, April 2021

Back Bay Books is an imprint of Little, Brown and Company, a division of Hachette Book Group, Inc. The Back Bay Books name and logo are trademarks of Hachette Book Group, Inc.

The publisher is not responsible for websites (or their content) that are not owned by the publisher.

The Hachette Speakers Bureau provides a wide range of authors for speaking events. To find out more, go to hachettespeakersbureau.com or call (866) 376-6591.

The following stories were previously published in a different form: "How to Pronounce Knife" in *Granta*; "Slingshot" in *Harper's*, *The O. Henry Prize Stories 2019*, and *Lit Hub*; "The Universe Would Be So Cruel" in *The Best American Non-Required Reading* and *NOON*; "Paris" in *Ricepaper Magazine* and *The Journey Prize Stories 28*; "Mani Pedi" in *The Puritan* and *The Journey Prize Stories 28*; "The School Bus Driver" in *NOON*; "Ewwrrrkk" as "Ewwrrrk!" in *Joyland*; "The Gas Station" in *The Paris Review*; "You Are So Embarrassing" in *The New Quarterly*; "Chick-A-Chee!" in *The Literary Review and Postcolonial Text*; and "Picking Worms" as "Worms" in *Ploughshares*.

ISBN 978-0-316-42213-0 (hc) / 978-0-316-42212-3 (pb)
LCCN 2019948532

Printing 1, 2021

LSC-C

Printed in the United States of America

To Mom and Dad and John,
for being here

Contents

How to Pronounce Knife

THE NOTE HAD BEEN typed out, folded over two times, and pinned to the child's chest. It could not be missed. And as she did with all the other notes that went home with the child, her mother removed the pin and threw it away. If the contents were important, a phone call would be made to the home. And there had been no such call.

The family lived in a small apartment with two rooms. On the wall of the main room was a tiny painting with a brown bend at the centre. That brown bend was supposed to be a bridge, and the blots of red and orange brushed in around it were supposed to be trees. The child's father had painted this, but he didn't paint anymore. When he came home from work, the first thing he always did was kick off his shoes. Then he'd hand over a newspaper to the child, who unfolded sheets on the floor, forming a square, and around that square they sat down to have dinner.

For dinner, it was cabbage and chitterlings. The butcher either threw the stuff away or had it out on display for cheap, so the child's mother bought bags and bags from him and put them in the fridge. There were so many ways to cook these: in a broth with ginger and noodles, grilled over charcoal fire, stewed with fresh dill, or the way the child liked them best—baked in the oven with lemongrass and salt. When she took these dishes to school, other children would tease her about the smell. She shot back, "You wouldn't know a good thing even if five hundred pounds of it came and sat on your face!"

When they all sat down for dinner, the child thought of the notes her mother threw away, and about bringing one to her father. There had been so many last week, maybe it was important. She listened as her father worried about his pay and his friends and how they were all making their living here in this new country. He said his friends, who were educated and had great jobs in Laos, now found themselves picking worms or being managed by pimple-faced teenagers. They'd had to begin all over again, as if the life they led before didn't count.

The child got up, found the note in the garbage, and brought it to her father.

He waved the note away. "Later." He said this in Lao. Then, as if remembering something important, he added, "Don't speak Lao and don't tell anyone you are Lao. It's no good to tell people where you're from." The child looked at the centre of her father's chest, where, on this T-shirt, four letters stood side by side: LAOS.

A FEW DAYS AFTER THAT, there was some commotion in the classroom. All the girls showed up wearing different variations of pink, and the boys had on dark suits and little knotted ties. Miss Choi, the grade one teacher, was wearing a purple dress dotted with a print of tiny white flowers and shoes with little heels. The child looked down at her green jogging suit. The green was dark, like the green of broccoli, and the fabric at the knees was a few shades lighter and kept their shape even when she was standing straight up. In this scene of pink and sparkles and matching purses and black bow ties and pressed collars, she saw she was not like the others.

Miss Choi, always scanning the room for something out of place, noticed the green that the child was wearing and her eyes widened. She came running over and said, "Joy. Did you get your parents to read the note we sent home with you?"

"No," she lied, looking at the floor where her blue shoes fitted themselves inside the space of a small square tile. She didn't want to lie, but there was no point in embarrassing her parents. The day went as planned. And in the class photo, the child was seated a little off to the side, with the grade and year sign placed in front of her. The sign was always right in the middle of these photos, but the photographer had to do something to hide the dirt on the child's shoes. Above that sign, she smiled.

When her mother came to get her after school, she asked why all the other children were dressed up this way, but the child didn't tell her. She lied, saying in Lao, "I don't know. Look at them, all fancy. It's just an ordinary day."

THE CHILD CAME HOME with a book. It was for her to read on her own, for practice. The book the child was given had pictures and a few words. The pictures were supposed to explain what was going on with the words, but there was this one word that didn't have a picture. It was there on the page by itself, and when she pronounced each letter, the word didn't sound like anything real. She didn't know how to pronounce it.

After dinner, the three of them sat down together on the bare floor, watching television side by side. From behind, the child knew she looked like her father. Her hair had been cut short in the shape of a bowl. The child's shoulders drooped and her spine bent like there was some weight she was carrying there, like she knew what a day of hard work was all about. Before long the television pictures changed into vertical stripes the colour of a rainbow, and her parents would soon go to bed. Most nights, the child followed, but tonight she was bothered by what she didn't know and wanted to know it. She opened the book and went looking for that word. The one that didn't sound like anything she knew.

That one.

It was her last chance before her father went to sleep. He was the only one in their home who knew how to read. She brought the book to him and pointed to the word, asked what it was. He leaned over it and said, "Kah-nnn-eye-ffff. It's kahneyff." That's what it was, what it sounded like to him.

THE NEXT DAY, Miss Choi gathered the whole class together to sit around the green carpet at the front of the room. She did this when she wanted to get someone to read out loud. Sometimes a student would volunteer and sometimes she would point at someone, but on this day Miss Choi looked around and found the child.

"Joy, you haven't read yet. Why don't you get your book and read for us."

The child started reading and everything went along just fine until she got to that word. It was only five letters, but there might as well have been twenty there. She said it the way her father had told her, but she knew it was wrong because Miss Choi would not turn the page. Instead, she pointed to the word and tapped at the page as if by doing so the correct sound would spill out. But the child didn't know how to pronounce it.

Tap. Tap. Tap. Finally, a yellow-haired girl in the class called out, "It's *knife*! The *k* is silent," and rolled her eyes as if there was nothing easier in the world to know.

This girl had blue eyes and freckles dotted around her nose. This girl's mother was always seen in the parking lot after school honking in a big shiny black car with a *V* and a *W* holding each other inside a circle. Her mother owned a black fur coat and walked in heels like it was Picture Day every day. This girl was like everyone else in the class, reading loud and clear, winning prizes. The child was the only one not to have won one yet. On this very day, Miss Choi added a red yo-yo to the sack. Had the child known what that word was, that red yo-yo would have been hers, but now it would remain locked in the top drawer of Miss Choi's desk.

LATER THAT NIGHT, the child looks over at her father during dinner. How he picks up each grain of rice with his chopsticks, not dropping a single one. How he eats, clearing away everything in his bowl. How small and shrunken he seems.

The child does not tell him the *k* in *knife* is silent. She doesn't tell him about being in the principal's office, about being told of rules and how things are the way they are. It was just a letter, she was told, but that single letter, out there alone, and in the front, was why she was in the office in the first place. She doesn't tell how she had insisted the letter *k* was not silent. It couldn't be, and she had argued and argued, "It's in the front! The first one! It should have a sound!" and then she screamed as if they had taken some important thing away. She never gave up on what her father said, on that first sound there. And none of them, with all their lifetimes of reading and good education, could explain it.

As she watches her father eat his dinner, she thinks of what else he doesn't know. What else she would have to find out for herself. She wants to tell her father that some letters, even though they are there, we do not say them, but she decides now is not the time to say such a thing. Instead she tells her father only that she had won something.

At the end of the school day, Miss Choi was waiting for her by the door. She asked the child to follow her to the front desk, where she unlocked the top drawer and pulled out the red velvet sack. "Pick one," she said. And the child reached inside and grabbed at the first thing her fingers touched. It was a puzzle with an airplane in the sky.

When she shows her father the prize, he is delighted because, in some way, he has won it too. They take the prize, all the little pieces of it, and start forming the edge, the blue sky, the other pieces, the middle. The whole picture, they fill those in later.

Paris

THE SKY WAS BLACK like the middle of an eye. Red revved the engine, impatient, having to wait for the truck to warm up. She never failed to make her morning shift on time. The truck was an old thing. A thing she had seen on someone's front lawn, a For Sale sign taped to the windshield, handwritten in black marker. The make was nothing special. They call it a pickup truck, but she never picked anything up in it, just herself. It might have been the colour that drew Red to the truck. And the thought of that big red truck in the parking lot at the plant. It would be the best-looking thing there, and it would belong to her. She wanted that.

Red worked at the plant like most of the others in town. It was her job to pluck the feathers, make sure the chickens were smooth when they left her. By the time the chickens got to her, they were already dead, their eyes closed tight like they were sleeping. It was almost like what happened in the next room didn't happen at all. Sometimes she could swear she heard the chickens—that sudden desperate flap of wing, as if flight could really take place there.

Before Red backed out onto the road, she looked at herself in the rear-view mirror. It didn't show her whole face, just the eyes. She lifted herself up from the driver's seat, turned her head to the right, studied the outline of her profile, and tried to imagine her face with a different nose. How maybe if her nose was different, things would be different at the plant too. Especially with Tommy. Tommy was her boss, her supervisor, married with two young boys. He was nice to her. Gave her more shifts than anyone else and complimented her work.

"You did good, Red. Keep it up. We've got plans for you."

What those plans were, she never knew. Just that they had them for her. Sometimes Tommy would buy her a cola from the machine or sit at her table during her lunch breaks. It wasn't how he behaved with the other girls who worked for him. There was no interest in her body. He didn't notice what was there, didn't lean in close or whisper anything. They talked. Mostly about his boys and how he was planning a trip to Paris with his wife for Valentine's Day.

Tommy's wife, Nicole, had a nose Red wished she could have. It was a thin nose that stuck out from her face and pointed upward. Everyone who worked in the front office had that kind of nose.

Nicole always came to the plant's annual Christmas party wearing something fashionable, in fabric no one else's clothes were made out of. The material fit tightly around her curves, smoothed out and pressed, not a wrinkle in sight. At these parties, Nicole always stood the whole time in a group with the other wives whose husbands ran or owned the company. This was the one occasion in the year their wives were seen, brought out for show. Sometimes one of them would come over to say hello to a couple of people who worked on the line. They would introduce themselves, shake a few hands, and then go back to stand in a corner with the other wives, as if they'd done some great charity work by breaking away from their huddle. Nicole never came over.

Every year at the party they served fried chicken. It never bothered Red that the pieces she ate could have been from one of those dead chickens that came to her to get plucked. Cut up into pieces like that, there wasn't a face to think of. And every year, she looked forward to this party, wore her best clothes to it: a pair of jeans, a blue-and-white checkered shirt, and thick black boots from Canadian Tire. Her clothes weren't fancy like what some of the other girls wore, and they didn't show much, but there wasn't much Red wanted to show.

A few years ago, one of the girls who worked on the line got a nose job. Her glasses didn't have to be held up with an elastic band at the back of the head anymore. The girl got her hair done after that, every week. She already had a small, thin body. "Cute" was what Tommy called it. Soon, she started getting more shifts and, eventually, a job in the front office. The front office! In this town, a girl either worked at the chicken plant or the Boobie Bungalow. At least at the Boobie Bungalow you could make some quick cash and get the hell out of town, never look back, or you could get someone who could love you just long enough to take you away. Any man you met there was single or on his way to being single. At the plant, most of the men were married, and if they weren't they would be eventually, to someone who didn't work there.

Red knew, for her, it was going to be the chicken plant. She didn't have much in the chest area, and couldn't dance to music even if it had a beat. The way men never looked at her gave her the sense that the Boobie Bungalow wasn't going to be an option for her. At the plant, you made enough money to pay for what you needed. But the big things in life, the things that could make you happy, well, you just never made enough to get all that.

About two years back, the girl who worked in the front office had stood with Tommy's wife and the other wives at the company Christmas party as if she was now one of them. All their noses looked the same, sticking out in the air like that. The wives didn't talk to the girl or include her in their conversations. When the group laughed together, her laughter came a few seconds behind.

But the girl doesn't work in the front office anymore. Something about Nicole and the other wives not liking her there, working with their husbands. She was asked to take her old job on the line again. She quit after that, on account of having been someplace better.

After the front office job became available again, all the women who worked on the line did what they could to get it. Some started by getting themselves nose jobs. Where they found a surgeon was something Red didn't know. No facility around here to support that kind of thing. Maybe that's why everyone's nose looked different: some were slightly bent, didn't heal properly, or scarred badly. One girl, when she talked, her nose moved in every direction that her upper lip moved. It was like her nose was attached to that lip. Most of the girls at the plant started to come to work with their hair curled and pressed and wearing heels and office clothes. They'd change into their work gear, the plastic shower cap and the matching white plastic pullover, then change right back when their shift was over. They looked so glamorous. But all of this was for nothing. None of them got the job. It was given to a girl just out of high school whose father worked in the front office.

RED DROVE HER TRUCK into the plant's parking lot and pulled up to a spot near the entrance. There was one closer, but it was reserved for those who worked in the front office. She didn't want to park where she did and imagined the day when she'd see her big red truck up there. She turned off the ignition and got out and walked to the entrance.

Somboun was standing outside alone, smoking. When he saw her coming, he dropped his cigarette and put it out with his shoe. Then he blew into his palm to check his breath and yelled out, "Hey, Dang!" Dang was what people who knew Red called her. It means *red* in Lao. It wasn't her real name, just a nickname she got because her nose was always red from the cold. She hated that he called her by a nickname. It made things feel intimate between them in a way she didn't want. The way he said "Dang," it was like a light in him had been turned on and now she had to be responsible for what he could see about himself.

Wherever she was in the plant, if he was around he would head straight toward her, excited and hopeful for something to happen between them. He was there when she punched in her time card, there at the end of the day when she punched out. He followed her around as if she were carrying feed. She wondered how he never got tired of smiling so much. She would look away from him, uninterested, but he would follow her gaze. He had seen her interest in the girls who got nose jobs, had seen her taking in how everyone else was noticing them too.

"I just don't see what the big deal is," he had said. "Why go and do that to your face for?"

"She's beautiful."

"But it's not real."

"It's real to her."

"I don't see it. I just don't."

"I want to get one too, you know," Red had confessed, before she realized she should not have said that to Somboun. Now that he knew she wanted something for herself, he might think he was some kind of friend to her.

"No. Not you. Not you. No way."

"Why not me? You think I don't want to be beautiful?"

"Why in hell would you do that to yourself! You're already beautiful." Somboun said this with such sincere conviction that she was embarrassed for him. How naked and bare, his want.

"How would you know. You don't know about girls."

Somboun lowered his head and quietly said, "I don't got to know anything about girls to know what's beautiful." He was so proud, and all for nothing. He'd worked at the plant the longest. Started when he was in high school, thinking this was something that was going to get him to college. Ten years later, he was still working at the plant doing the same thing. He was the one who slit the necks in the other room before they got to Red. He saw the chickens when they were still alive. She shuddered at the thought of doing anything with Somboun. What kind of gentleness could a man who did that for a living be capable of?

Still, after that, nose jobs were the one thing Somboun could manage to get Red to talk to him about. Who had got a nose job and when and if it was a good one. Red told him she was going to get a nose job too as soon as she saved up enough. She always said, "Next year, for sure. For sure."

When Red saw Somboun standing at the entrance that morning, still smoking even though he often talked about quitting, and wearing the same drab uniform and the same haircut all these years, he reminded her of all the things she wanted for herself but still didn't have. Day after day, the sight of him in the same place and in the same clothes and giving her the same greeting each morning showed that, for them, nothing had changed. Nothing had happened.

"I didn't get one!" she yelled at him.

"You look fine the way you are," he said, as if they were just picking up a conversation where they'd left off. As if the only time that counted for him were the ones they spent together, talking.

Walking quickly past him, she said, "Thanks, *Sam.*" Red knew he hated to be called by his English name. "Not Sam," he would insist, "Somboun," pronouncing the tones of the vowels the way Lao people would, refusing to make it easy. But he took what she said as if she was teasing and he smiled widely. To know someone's dislikes was to be close to them.

"Hey, Dang?" Somboun called after her, trying to hold her attention and to keep up with her as she entered the plant.

"What is *it*?" Red said irritably, hoping not to encourage him further.

"Did you hear about Khet? It was cancer. Started a few months after her nose job. Might have something to do with the material they put in there." Somboun was always coming up with reasons as to why a nose job was a bad idea. "Just something to think about," he said, grinning as if the cancer was a blessing in disguise, opening up an opportunity for him to talk with Red.

She walked faster and he soon fell behind.

IT WAS TIME to break for lunch. They only got twenty minutes. Enough time to use the washroom and gobble down some food. Red often used the time to be alone. The smell of raw chicken flesh and loosened guts and all that killing and packaging sometimes made her forget she was alive and living in the world too. She was on her way out of the line when she saw Tommy come by and tap the shoulder of one of the girls who worked for him. This was something he often did. That girl was the one selected for that day. Red made her way outside. A short time later, Tommy and the girl came out and walked to his car, where all of it took place. Red wondered what that felt like, to be seen, to feel the mouth of someone who wanted you. It didn't matter if what Tommy did wasn't for forever. He did it and you got to be something to him for a little while.

Just as they were getting into the car, Tommy's wife pulled into the parking lot.

She didn't even bother to park properly.

Nicole wore a white fur coat, her blond curls bounced fresh from the salon. She had bright red lipstick on and rouged cheeks. She looked so glamorous and beautiful.

She was yelling at him about something. Furious.

Then Nicole grabbed Tommy by the arm. He pulled his arm back and shoved her away. She didn't fall. She clung to a sleeve, her white heels dragging in the snow. What she wanted didn't matter to Tommy. He shut the door and drove away with the girl in the car. The bottom of Nicole's white fur coat was dirty with mud. If Red had not seen the whole thing, she might have thought the mud was shit. Might have asked how the shit got all over her like that.

From where Red stood, she could tell Nicole's eyes were smeared with mascara, and her quivering lips looked a clownish red now. Women like Nicole are who the romantic movies were made for. They are always the star of their own lives and they always got their man in the end. But beauty, for all it could get you and all that fussing it took to get it, seemed so awful a burden to have to carry and maintain. There was so much to lose. In that moment, Red felt grateful for what she was to others—ugly. It's one thing to be ugly and not know it. It's another to know.

That public declaration of love in front of family and friends like Nicole and Tommy had—Red knew it wasn't something that would ever happen for her. It didn't matter what Tommy did outside of that promise. It had been made, and he would always come back to it sooner or later.

The only love Red knew was that simple, uncompli- cated, lonely love one feels for oneself in the quiet moments of the day. It was there, steady and solid in the laughter and talk of the television and with her in the grocery aisles on the weekends. It was there every night, in the dark, spectacular and sprawling in the quiet. And it all belonged to her.

Nicole spotted Red and ran to her. She grabbed Red and held her like they were the closest of friends, and buried her pointy nose in Red's neck. She could feel the poke. Nicole probably would have grabbed on to anyone standing there. Probably. They stood there together in each other's arms. It was the first time someone had ever been that close to Red, had touched her. Both women cried, but for different reasons.

Slingshot

I WAS SEVENTY when I met Richard. He was thirty-two. He told me he was a young man, and I didn't say anything about that because I really didn't know what that was, to be a young man, if that was a good thing to be or a bad one. He had moved in next door to us, me and Rose, my granddaughter, in January. She was hardly home that summer. She had gotten together with a new guy and was mostly at his place across town.

Richard had parties every Saturday. At first, it was just the housewarming, and then it was other things. His apartment door was always open, people coming in and out at all hours. Sometimes there were just kids over there, little ones, playing with Christmas lights, shaping them into small sculptures, leaving a mess of wire and bulbs on the floor. Other times it was middle-aged people crawling through some tent maze built out of cardboard boxes. He even had a party where people brought over their bikes, and we took a tour of the city. I did not have a bike, so he let me ride with him. I sat on the bar in front of the seat and he pedalled. He told us stories, personal ones, about his time living here. He'd been in the city for a few years. On the bike tour, he told us about a woman he'd loved once. He showed us where they ate and skipped out on a bill, the places they kissed. There was something about the way he told this story. The city became his. Later, when I walked by that building, that corner, his stories were there. His gloomy voice played in my head like an old record.

"THERE'S NO SUCH THING as love. It's a construct," Richard told me one day when I went over to his apartment. I had gotten a package of his in my mailbox. "You know anyone who is in love?"

I thought of Rose, who always said she was in love whenever she met a new guy and then would wait by the phone all day, crying. Then I thought of my friends and my own experience. We had all known love, but it happened a long time ago. It was not something we sat around wondering about. It happened, and when it's happened, there is no need to think too hard about it.

I said, "Maybe you haven't had enough time to know a range of people."

He told me he knew a lot of people. Thousands was the number he gave me. I wanted to tell him we were talking about different things, but I wasn't sure he'd understand. A few minutes passed between us, and then he said, "People say that they're in love all the time, but they're not. I don't believe them. They think they should say it because it's what you say. Doesn't mean they really know what it is."

I looked around his apartment. There wasn't much in it. A couple of chairs, a couch he'd dragged back from someone's front lawn, a table, and a little anatomy man. The anatomy man had plastic bits inside. I reached inside him and took out a small brown thing the size of a pencil eraser. I didn't know what it was and put it back.

RICHARD LIKED TO TALK about the women he had slept with. There were two he brought up a lot. The first was his ex-roommate, the one he told us about on the bike tour. The second was a woman named Eve. She lived in New York now but came back once in a while to visit. He said he wasn't in love with her, that they were just best friends. They had, for seven years, been a couple, but now they weren't. The chemistry wasn't there anymore. When she didn't answer his emails or phone calls, he would google her.

I asked him, "Do you think maybe you're still in love with her?" He said no—to be in love, you should want to have sex with that person, and he didn't want that with her. He asked me if I'd had sex with anyone lately. I took my time to answer. I could tell he had no use for anyone who didn't have sex. I tried to remember the last time. I hadn't been with anyone but my husband. He died thirty years ago. A heart attack. Sudden. Thirty years is a lifetime for some people. As far as I was concerned, I hadn't had sex for such a long time that I could consider myself a virgin again. I couldn't remember how it all happens.

Richard knew how. He was always talking about the sex he'd had. With hundreds of women, he told me.

"It's easy. You just ask. And you never know. If someone tells me no, I don't get worked up about it. I mean, they said no. What's more clear than that? There are always others who want to. It's sometimes just fun to do it. Doesn't have to mean anything." Richard was not a beauty, but he acted like one. He said, "I'm not bad-looking. Anyway, looks don't have anything to do with it. Sometimes good-looking people don't do anything in bed. They just lie there. You want someone who has imagination, who is excited. It's the best feeling ever."

RICHARD HAD ONE of his parties. This party was different from the others. There wasn't any food, and it began later in the evening. There was a green glass bottle on the floor in the middle of the room. All his furniture had been cleared away and piled on one side of the room. For all his talk, I had never seen him with a woman before. I knew what the bottle was for.

I looked around the room, at the twenty-five or so people gathered, to see if there was anyone I hoped it would land on. There wasn't, but I still wanted to play. When I spun the bottle, it landed on a beautiful blond woman. A lawyer. She was still in her business suit, with the jacket on. I kissed her on the forehead, like she was some child, and everyone laughed. Richard said, "Isn't she sweet?" I hated that he said that. I didn't want to be sweet. I was old and I knew it and I had been called a lot of things, but "sweet" really irritated me. I watched as those who were chosen by the bottle kissed each other. After a while, it got boring. The people at the party thought so too and started to file out. I don't remember who else was playing, or who they kissed. I only wanted it to be Richard's turn. And each time it was, he always spent a long time with that person, kissing. He kissed a man who had a heavy belly, and then a dancer, then several others. He kissed them all with the same tenderness.

Richard told me, "You could go home, if you want. We're just going to keep playing this game. It might get boring." But I didn't want to go home yet. It was the start of summer and I wanted something to happen to me.

There were three of us now. The other woman was named Lorrie. She worked in an art gallery. Lorrie behaved like she was a girl—giggling, chewing a few strands of her long hair, blushing. When Richard spun the green bottle this time, it landed on me. He laughed and said, "You don't have to. You can say no." But I didn't want to say no. He was sitting crossed-legged on the floor, and I leaned over. He chewed spearmint gum. When we stopped, she was gone.

He said, "It's three in the morning. You should go home." He said it like a good friend who was looking out for me. I got the sense too that Richard didn't like me being there at that time, alone with him. As though he was afraid of what an old woman wanted. "I don't want to," I said. I don't know why I said it. Maybe just to see what he would do. He was a man, and I was bored.

His bedroom was clean and quiet. I said, "Can you take off your clothes? I want to see." It surprised me, how he listened. He didn't say it was a bad idea. He stood there naked, and he was beautiful, the way women are. He had hair on his chest and legs. I hadn't seen hair on a chest for a long time and so I reached out to touch it. He closed his eyes and breathed deeply. It was so easy. He sat down on the bed and I sat on top of him. He didn't go in deep but held me there. I was supposed to lower myself. But I didn't. I could go as far as I wanted. The morning light came in, and he said, "We have to stop." I didn't want to. I liked looking at Richard's face when he held me there. He looked scared, or like he was about to cry. Then he lifted me off him and turned around so I couldn't see his face. He said, "You have to go. I want to fuck you." And that's why I didn't want to go. Because he wanted that.

———

AFTER THAT NIGHT, I didn't see Richard for a few weeks. He had his parties and people came and went. I heard their talk through the walls, and the women too. I wanted to know what it would feel like to have a sound like that in my mouth. But it was only ever the women I heard. He was silent, breathing quietly, probably.

I asked him why he never made any noises, not even a grunt. "I'm concentrating," he said. He always talked that way. Easily. He told me what it felt like, for him, for a man, and what it was like having sex with a woman. I had never known that. He told me things I wished my mother could have told me. I wanted to know how he talked to a woman, how he got them to come home to his apartment, how he undressed them, how he knew where to put himself, if it was the same each time. He always asked them, Can I do this? Is this all right? You're okay with this? The way he described it to me, it was like I had done it too, like I had also been inside them, just like him, as a man. There was no metaphor, no seed and soil and growing flowers. Just the facts.

AFTER ROSE LEFT for the weekend, I knocked on Richard's door. I tried the doorknob and went in.

I could hear the shower going, and when he came out, he said, "You hungry?" Just like that. As if he'd expected me all along. He was a good cook. I watched him bringing out plates, the pan, opening the cupboards, the fridge.

I liked that he wasn't mad at me for what happened last time, when we had gotten so close. "Why would I be?" he said. "Don't have sex with men who get mad about things like that." He smiled at me and said, "I liked that nothing really happened. We were close. That's the best part. To be that close. And to let nothing happen."

Soon after, we were sitting on the edge of his bed. I sat on top and I had Richard between my legs. I kissed him. It started off really slow and gentle. And then I kissed harder. Then he pulled his mouth away from mine. His mouth was open, and he was breathing heavily. His head tilted back when I leaned forward. We were so close, breathing into each other's mouths. Then I lowered myself onto him and said, before I pushed further, "Do you want me to pull out?" I meant stop, but he knew what I meant and why I didn't say that. He laughed and said, "No, no. God, no." His lips were red, his cheeks pink. "Tell me you love me," I said. "Even if it's not true. Say it." And he did. I wanted to feel what it was like to have someone inside me again, and so I pushed him into me.

IT WAS THE END of August, and Richard didn't have his parties as often. We were spending more time together alone. He'd call me on the phone and ask whether I wanted to come over. I knew what he wanted me over for, and I wanted that too. I went over whenever he called. Sometimes we spent the whole day together, not talking at all. We didn't have much to say, doing what we did. What I liked about the sex we had was how slow it was, and how long we could go, how he waited for my body to respond. When we began it was usually dark outside, and then we stopped when there was light. He told me, "You should get a boyfriend. I can't be your boyfriend." But I didn't want a boyfriend, whatever that was these days. I wanted what I had. I didn't say anything. I just watched him put on his clothes. Then he turned to me and asked if I wanted to go with him to see his friend, Eve, the next day. She was in town, and she wanted him to meet her new boyfriend. He said he didn't want to go alone.

THE NEXT MORNING, I stood on the front porch of a house on a small street, and Richard went inside to get Eve. She was at the back of the house, where the kitchen was. She called to me to come inside, waved me in. She had long, shiny black hair and brown eyes. She said her boyfriend was upstairs taking a shower and that he'd join us in a few minutes. Richard talked to Eve, asked her about this new man of hers, teased her about him, about being in love.

Then Richard said, "Well, I'm in love," and pointed to me. "With her." We laughed, Richard and I, as if this was our joke and Eve was outside it. You can do that with a joke, hide how you feel and mean what you say at the same time, and no one will ask you which it is.

Eve's boyfriend, Daniel, came down the stairs in plain khaki shorts and a white T-shirt that clung to his chest. "Hey, guys, how is everyone?" Richard answered for himself. I didn't reply, and it didn't seem to matter. They moved on.

For the rest of the morning, we played board games and charades. Eve and Richard had a way of talking with each other that made it difficult to join in. They made references and jokes and told stories about each other in bits and pieces that never came together because they'd break out in laughter. They never bothered to explain what any of this was about, always saying we would have had to be there to get it. I had been around. I knew what was happening. Richard was oblivious to what Eve was doing with him. Playing the two men off each other.

I got up and went out to the front porch. It was only three in the afternoon. I thought of going home, and then Daniel came out for a smoke. He lit his cigarette and we watched the trees around us. The leaves were far apart and they waved, darted left and right. Pushed by the wind, they looked like a school of fish in the blue sky. A thing out of place. We did not know what to say to each other. We were there at the same time, wanting the same thing but from different people. If there were anyone else who understood what it was like to be on the outside looking in on those two, it was Daniel.

After a while, he said to me, "You ever seen a tornado before?" I told him I hadn't. He nodded and went on,

"They destroy everything. You can see it coming in the distance. Most people would try to get the hell out of there. Some people see it coming and can't help but watch." I didn't say anything. And then he winked at me.

AFTERWARDS, RICHARD THOUGHT it would be a great idea to bike around the city. Eve and Daniel didn't want to go, so it was just the two of us again. We arranged our bodies on the bike like we had done once before, me on the bar in front of the seat while he pedalled. We went around like this, without helmets. I wasn't scared of getting into an accident. That's what it felt like then, to be with Richard. I didn't think about what would happen to me, what the future would look like. I was in it.

Richard biked past the crowd at the ferry dock, and we followed the trail out of the city until we got to the lake. We weren't supposed to swim in it because the water was polluted, but he did, saying there was nothing wrong. He swam far out but close enough for me to see him pretend he was drowning. His arms waved about and his head bobbed. Then he swam out farther and did it all over again.

When we returned to his apartment, he told me his friendship with Eve was changing. She was getting on with her life, without him. She didn't drop everything to see him anymore. "I should marry her," he said. "I love her and I don't want to lose her." I did not tell him what to do about her. I did not ask what it would mean for me.

He took off his clothes, then mine. The afternoon had changed him somehow. He had always been very tender with me but was even more so now. He lay himself down on the bed and closed his eyes. I took him in. I did it slowly. "Yes," he said. I wanted to put something inside him that we could both see go in and out. I put a finger into his belly button, and he got so loud about it, like the women I heard him with through the wall of the apartment. I was quiet, breathing, taking everything in. Then he gasped like something was about to happen to him. He sat up and pulled me closer. He kissed me very hard and did not pull away. We continued like that, face to face. I love you, he kept saying.

He asked me to sleep over, but I didn't want to. I watched him with a sadness he couldn't see. I didn't want to be with someone who could do that—who could deny what I was. He had the time to have regrets, to be stupid. I didn't. And when he turned away from me, I don't know why I did what I did. I reached out and grabbed a piece from inside the anatomy man. It was his stomach. A small plastic thing. It wasn't real, of course, but it was there, and it was something.

I went home and was surprised to find Rose there. She asked me where I had been, said she knew that I was spending a lot of time with that guy next door. She said, "He's never going to love you, you know. Have you

forgotten how old you are? Look at all your wrinkles."
That's the thing about being old. We don't know we
have wrinkles until we see them. Old is a thing that happens on the outside. A thing other people see about us.
I didn't know why she was talking to me this way. Maybe
it had nothing, really, to do with me. I didn't say anything. It seemed to me she'd been drinking, so I let her
talk. After a while, I didn't hear anything she said.

I DID SEE RICHARD one last time, later that year, in
October. It was at Daniel's funeral. Richard was there,
with Eve, supporting her, holding her, like a partner. It
seemed strange to me to see him go back to her. And
it seemed strange to me for us to have done the things
people who loved each other did, and for it to seem now
like none of it had ever happened. But it was not just
him. What kind of person was Eve, to see someone else's
love and agree to see it wasn't there. But after a while, it
didn't matter.

I looked over at the closed casket and thought of what
I'd read in the newspaper about Daniel, how he died. He
was a strong swimmer, in excellent shape, but it had
been very cold, and he must have gotten a cramp, and
drowned. I thought of him and his whole life, how short
it was. Forty. That isn't much time. I was there with him
when he loved someone, and he was willing to wait it out.
I wondered whether, in life, you get one big role, some

message you need to deliver to someone, and when it's done, it's time to go. I thought of what Daniel had said about tornadoes. He was wrong about me. We weren't the same. I did not wait. I am not the kind of person who watches something happen in the distance.

Daniel's family and friends stood up and told stories about him. I did not tell mine. It was for no one to know, and I left. I looked back at the black everyone was wearing. I could not tell which figure in the crowd was Richard. I was beginning to forget his face.

ONCE, WHEN I was walking down the street in front of my old building, Richard called out to me. I must have been closing in on eighty then. I looked through him and spun around. I wanted to be in the distance, beautiful and dark, spinning all by myself, in the clear. I didn't want him to come close. Nothing, not even the call of my name, could make me stop.

Randy Travis

THE ONLY THING my mother liked about the new country we were living in was its music. We had been given a small radio as part of the welcome package from the refugee settlement program. There were other items in the box, such as snow pants, mittens, and new underwear, but it was the radio she cherished most. A metal box with a dial that picked up a few channels. The volume button had only three ticks, and then it couldn't go any farther to the right. She held this little radio up to her ear like a seashell and listened. The host always spoke briefly between songs and there was the occasional laugh. A laugh, in any language, was a laugh. His laugh was gentle and private and welcoming. You got the sense that he, too, was alone somewhere. Grateful for the sound of a human voice and for the music that kept her company, she listened to the radio constantly while I was at school and my father was at work.

My mother especially loved American country music, because it reminded her of the way the women in her family talked among themselves. It felt familiar. The pleas, the gossip, the dreams of the big city, what it was like to come from a place no one had ever heard of. The songs always told a story you could follow—ones about heartbreak, or about love, how someone can promise to love you forever and ever and ever, Amen. My mother did not know what *Amen* meant, but she guessed it was something you said at the end of a sentence to let people know the sentence was finished. "Three apples, Amen," she would say at the corner grocery store. Because of this, our neighbours thought my mother was religious, and even though our family was Buddhist, she caught a ride to church with them every Sunday. She made friends easily, was quick to smile, and was never shy about practising her English.

At church, she told us they ate one cracker and took one swallow of red wine and the rest of the time there was a man talking. She did not know exactly what he said, but he said it for a long time. Sometimes, just to give her hands something to do, she would pick up the heavy book in front of her seat and open it. Even though she didn't understand everything they were singing, she moved her lips anyway. It was just like at the citizenship ceremony. Whether or not you understood the oath you made, you had to move your lips.

After a while, for some reason she seemed to lose interest in going. She didn't say why.

WHEN MY FATHER got his first paycheque, he wanted to buy something that wasn't a necessity. We were living in a new country now. We could have grand ideas of owning something luxurious. My mother suggested a car so he wouldn't have to take a bus to work, but that was out of our price range. They thought of going to a fancy restaurant like the ones their friends took them to, but they did not like the way the steaks were cooked, thick slabs fried in butter. There was no fish sauce with hot spices and herbs at the table. They talked about getting a wooden bed frame to put their mattress on, but beds were for sleeping on, not for show. There were many things my father could have bought with his first paycheque, but in the end he decided on a record player. In Laos, it was something only rich people owned.

My mother loved the control the record player gave her. With the radio, she had to wait for what she wanted to hear. It could be days before she heard her favourite song again. Now she could drop the needle onto the black disc and watch it turn and turn, and listen to her favourite songs whenever she wanted. She never went back to the radio after that.

Later, once we could afford a TV and a VCR, she taped the country music award shows. After the nominations were read, she'd yell out her pick for the winner. If she got any wrong, she would memorize the winners in each category and replay the show and yell out the correct names. Whenever Dolly Parton was nominated, she chose her, and she was right every time. She'd yell, "I won!" I didn't understand why she did that. What she'd won was nothing but being right.

The songs my mother loved most were by Randy Travis. Whenever we saw a new Randy Travis music video on television, she would quickly hit the Record button, and everything else slipped from her mind. She would kneel with her face close to the screen, then reach over and hit Rewind and Play, watch him sing again and again. After a while, the labels on the buttons began to fade and disappear.

By then, she didn't care much for the things she usually did around the house. The laundry would be done but the clothes remained unfolded, dishes washed but not dried or put away. Then, she discovered frozen dinners. You could warm them up in minutes. And these dinners were my favourite for a time. It was what all my friends ate at home. I loved having mashed potatoes and corn and steak and roast chicken. My father did not. He wanted papaya salad, padaek, pickled cabbage, blood sausage, and sticky rice. But those dishes took days to prepare and getting the ingredients meant long bus rides to the market in Chinatown. It took time to ferment fish sauce, to pickle, to chop up a whole chicken into its parts, and to soak the rice to soften it. Time that my mother wanted to spend listening to Randy Travis sing.

My father was nothing like Randy Travis. No one noticed who he was or what he did for his living. He never used the word *love* or showed much sentiment. For my mother's birthday, he gave her a few twenty-dollar bills. Not even a birthday card or plans for a night out. He thought that because he was there, that was all that was needed to show his love. He thought his silence was love, his restraint was love. To say it out loud, to display it so openly, was to be shameless. He thought it was ridiculous to be moaning about love so much. What kind of man was Randy Travis, with his health, his looks, his fame, and his money, that he should ever have anything to cry about?

One morning, my mother gave me some money to buy one of those teen *Bop* magazines so we could find a mailing address for Randy Travis at the back of it. She brought out a card printed with a pink heart on the front, but because she couldn't read or write English, she told me to write a note to him for her. I did not know what to write. I must have been about seven. What could I know then about the language of adult love? While she curled a few strands of her hair around a finger and broke out in small fits of giggles, I stood there, unable to decide how to even begin a sentence to him. I didn't like how she was acting, and I was afraid of what would happen to my father if Randy Travis ever wrote back.

So I wrote, *I do not like you.*

My mother would never know what I had written.

I told her I'd written *I love you forever and ever,* just like his song.

She smiled, and then signed her name underneath.

We sent these cards to Randy Travis again and again, and though no one ever wrote back, my mother insisted we keep on sending them. I tried to think of what to write and thought of the things people wrote in the bathroom at school or spray-painted on the brick outside our building. *You're ugly. Go back home. Loser.* Sometimes I didn't even get the chance to write anything before she signed her name on the card, sealed it inside an envelope, and pushed it down into the dark slot of the mailbox at the corner of our street. We must have sent out hundreds of these cards, spending money on stamps and envelopes, my mother always hoping to get something back. It wasn't any different than what she had done to come to this country, she said.

Of course I told my father about what we were doing, thinking he could put a stop to her obsession. It was getting out of hand. By then I'd refused to help her anymore, saying I had homework, thinking this would stop the letters, but she kept mailing them on her own with just her name inside. I showed one of the cards to my father. He pointed to her signature. It looked like pretzels, loopy and knotted, and he laughed and said to my mother, "Randy Travis reads English. He's gonna look at your name and see a doodle. That address you got, who knows what they really do there. For all we know, the cards probably go straight to the dump."

But my mother continued to send those cards with her name written out in Lao. Randy Travis was all she could think of and talk about. When the pipe in the kitchen sink clogged and my father didn't know how to fix it, my mother said, "Oh, I bet Randy Travis knows how to do that." And then there was the time she said out loud over dinner, "I bet Randy Travis would like to have dinner with me." She'd stare outside the window at the sky, the moon, the sun, or a cloud and say, "Randy Travis could be looking at the very same thing I'm looking at right now. Wherever he is."

It was inevitable that my father got tired of hearing about Randy Travis, and he finally said to her, sadly, that the man was famous and that our lives would never cross his. "He doesn't even know we exist. We're not even a single glitter of light to him," he said. Then he brought his hand to his face, formed a circle around his eye with his fingers, and closed the space inside until there was nothing left except a tight fist. But you could not talk her out of her Randy Travis love. It was a shadow that covered her up, and all you could do was wait for some light to come through. She even started dressing up like Dolly Parton, thinking this was the kind of woman he'd want. She dyed her hair blond, teased its strands, and tied it in an upsweep. She played his music and sat by the window, waiting and gazing out onto the street below, as if he was going to drive up and take her away.

Hoping for some of this Randy Travis love to brush off on him, my father started wearing these cowboy boots my mother got for him at a garage sale. Pretty soon, he was wearing jeans and flannel tops, and standing like Randy Travis. He'd hook a thumb into the belt loop of his jeans and stand there with one leg straight and the other loose at the knee so it jutted forward. It made my mother happy to see him change in this way. But then when my mother asked him to sing, he failed spectacularly.

He did not know how to pronounce the words.

Her broad and hopeful smile vanished from her face, but my father only tried harder, belting out the chorus louder, holding on to the vowels, trying to produce a southern twang. He was no star. He was no leading man. He packed store furniture into cardboard boxes for a living. No one would pay to see him sing, but he didn't care. He was only trying to be what my mother wanted.

ONE DAY, MY father told me we were going to a Randy Travis concert. He said, "It's what your mother wants. We have to do this for her." He rented a car and we drove down south. In those days, there was no such thing as buying things online. You had to walk up to a concert venue and buy a ticket right there at the box office.

My mother was so thrilled, she made the kinds of food my father liked to eat. She spent the three days before we

set out soaking sticky rice, and when it was done cook-
ing, she put it in a thip khao and bundled that in a blanket
so it would keep its warmth. She made papaya salad and
crushed tiny dry shrimps into it, and fried up two quails
and wrapped them up in aluminum foil. I hadn't noticed
how beautiful Lao food was before. After the bland yellows
and browns of those TV dinners, it felt like a homecoming.
Arranged together, the colours were so bold and bright,
the flavours popped and sharpened. Every meal tasted like
a special occasion. It was a reminder of where she came
from and her love. I could now see why my father insisted
on eating nothing but this.

I do not remember much about the drive there except
seeing a blue-and-red sign with the number 75 on it. We
followed it for many days. I couldn't see much out the window. I only saw black wires like underlines in the blue of
the sky and then the dark and my own little face staring
back at me.

At the concert, we were so high up on the outer ring
of the audience I could not tell if it really was Randy
Travis onstage. His face was the size of a pin. I closed my
left eye and measured him with my thumb and index finger from where we were. He wasn't more than an inch
between my two fingers. And I don't know why, but I
closed that space he took up until I couldn't see him anymore. It was when he started to sing that I opened my
other eye and realized it had to be Randy Travis on that
stage. His voice matched exactly the one from our records.

He did not move around much onstage. He mostly just stood there, strumming his guitar. He actually seemed shy, casting his eyes to the ground whenever the crowd rose to their feet with applause. He'd nod to acknowledge their praise, then begin another song. He did not look at anyone in particular. Didn't single out anyone to sing to. He stared out into the crowd and the spotlight lit him with a glow I hadn't seen before. He seemed to sparkle. Once in a while, he would wave in our direction and my mother would wave back. But we were just a black dot in the dark to him. I thought of what it must have cost my father to bring us to this concert. The hours he put in lifting and packing all that furniture into homes we could never own ourselves. Homes owned by the kind of people who could afford to sit closer to Randy Travis. From where we were sitting, the stage lights lit up their heads so they gleamed.

After the concert, we waited with all the young teenage girls by the tour bus, but I was too small to see anything besides people's backsides. I saw my father reach for my mother's hand, but he missed. So he put both his hands in his pockets and looked to the ground, at his cowboy boots.

WHEN I THINK of it now, I'm not surprised that, a few years later, my mother would find something else to devote herself to. This time it was slot machines. She sat up close as those machines lit up her face and swallowed her hope coin by coin. I knew my mother was no stranger to hoping; it's how we all ended up here in this country in the first place. She got in the habit of not coming home, sleeping in the car most nights in the parking lot of some casino, my father waiting up to see if she'd come home. It wasn't long after that we were told she was found collapsed in the parking lot. People die sometimes, and there doesn't have to be a reason why. That's just the way life is.

It seems wrong to say, but I felt relief for her then.

LAST MONTH, it was my forty-second birthday. I went to visit my father in that old apartment. Everything was the same, except the view. There was a building now where there had once been a park. It had become a place where the light did not get in. My father took out his wallet, which was made of brown leather and frayed at the edges. It was packed with receipts, coins, and mints. He grabbed a bunch of twenty-dollar bills and held them out for me, but I waved the money away and said I didn't need it. He asked me if I had eaten and when I said I hadn't, he fried fish with grated ginger and brought out a plate of papaya salad and sticky rice. We didn't say much to each other. We were eating. I got choked up at the first taste of the papaya salad. Fermented fish sauce is like a fingerprint—you could trace who it belonged to by how it was made. My father added crabs to his sauce, which was thick and dark, fermenting for years. That wasn't how my mother made her sauce.

After dinner, my father and I went into the living room to watch television. He came upon the country music channel and there was a Randy Travis special on. We watched a few of his music videos and then my father got up and turned on his karaoke machine. I was nervous for him, cringing at the memory of how he had sung all those years ago, when he didn't know the lyrics or how to pronounce the words. Now, with the help of that machine, he knew what to do. I was the only one there, and I was sitting up close. The instruments started and a white dot hovered over the words. Then, he opened his mouth, and I was astonished.

Mani Pedi

THE BRIGHT INDUSTRIAL LIGHTS hung in neat rows on the ceiling. Raymond was alone in the dressing room. It's how you know you lost. He knew it would come to this. They only ever talked about winning and knockouts and the ways in which he didn't measure up. But, in his mind, the joy of boxing was in the small details no one was there to see. He loved what it took to get here— the routine, the training, the discipline. And the buildup before the fight, the few moments after he finished wrapping up his hands and put on his gloves, his heart racing, and before he entered the ring and touched gloves. Before anything had been decided about him, when the possibility that he might win this one—just this one time—was a chance as good as any and all he had to do was step into that opening. Even when that didn't happen, being in the ring still meant seeing a champion up close, becoming a small detail in his list of bouts. It meant he, Raymond, had been there.

And it was hearing his sister's voice in his corner that he loved the most. Raymond heard the excitement of the crowd, their chanting, screaming, and jeering. But no matter how loud they got, his sister's voice always broke through. The way she would cuss out the other guy or the audience when they turned on Raymond. He came from nothing, and to stand up anyway and to try for something—well, if that wasn't courage, he wasn't sure what was.

Raymond didn't know what had happened out there in the ring—a flurry of jabs and punches, and then he was out. At the time, none of that hurt. The pain came afterwards, and matched the sadness he carried around in him, anchored in his body like an extra set of bones. He knew he would lose even before the fight began. Knew it for sure once he was in the ring and he couldn't lift his arms or his head, couldn't see his opponent's face or understand what he was doing in the ring. He couldn't think out there. Couldn't move his feet fast enough, couldn't move out of the way when a punch came. They landed in the middle of his face. Quick, hard, sudden. He was trained to see them coming, but he just stood there like some fool waiting for them. When he played back tapes of the fights his sister had recorded for him, he saw the punches in slow motion, how the impact rippled across his nose, his cheekbones, his hair. And when it was over, he could see nothing but black light, those lit-tle dots that peppered everything in his vision. He knew it was about time for him to be through with fighting. He had to get it out of his mind that he could ever be a champ. Truth was, he had become what they call a trial horse. He was just there for someone to punch, a body to pass through on the way to some victory belt. He said he'd quit if it ever got to be like that, and it got to be like that. This wasn't the way he wanted to leave boxing, but it was over now, and he knew it.

Raymond wasn't the only person who'd ever lost the place he saw for himself in the world, but that's not how it felt to him then. He lived in a mouldy, cold basement with just one window. When he first got the place, he thought he would be able to see sky once in a while, but the floor wasn't down low enough so all he saw were shoes and boots and heels. Feet.

Raymond's sister did well for herself. She owned Bird Spa and Salon. The slogan was "Nails! Cheap! Cheap!" It was catchy. She wanted him to come work with her. She said he didn't have to go to school or nothing. He just had to listen to what she told him to do. It would be just like it was in the ring. She'd yell at him like he was in the corner and he'd just go out and get it done.

Instead, Raymond had gotten a job scooping out ice-cream flavours at the mall, and when that shift was over he started another one frying bland cabbage. He hadn't seen his sister in weeks. Hadn't called her or picked up the phone when she rang. But she wouldn't have that, him not calling her back, so one night she came over, worried about what he was becoming, what he was doing with his life. She was real dramatic about it. She had a key to his apartment and kicked open the door and beat him on the chest, her small fists hitting him like water droplets in the shower. She told him that even if he didn't want better for himself, she did. She brought up their dead parents—she always did that when she was desperate to make a meaningful point. She said they didn't leave Laos, a bombed-out country in a war no one ever heard of, "on a fucking raft made of bamboo to have you asking, 'You want sprinkles with that?'" She slapped him across the face. "Raymond, what you cook at the mall, I can vomit up shit better than that!" So he agreed to join her at the nail salon just to get her to calm down. Not long after that, he was answering the phones and saying, "Hello, Bird and Spa Salon. We do nails. Cheap! Cheap!"

At first he mopped the floor and refilled the bottles with nail polish remover, cuticle oil, or whatever was running low. He cut paper towels into neat little squares to save everyone time. He turned on the switch to keep the waxing oil hot. When all that got to be easy for him, his sister asked him to sit in and watch whenever the girls did manicures and pedicures or waxed an eyebrow or upper lip. It amazed him to see clients transformed. It was like what happened in the ring, but in reverse. They came in looking like they'd been through a few rounds, sad and exhausted, shoulders slumped, but left carefree and happy and refreshed. He thought of the injuries that happened to guys like him and what it did to the lives they had outside the ring—if you could even call it that. There was the guy who didn't wake up from a fight until a year later, and the guy who never got back his confidence, stopped training, ate doughnuts all day, threw away his whole career. Then there was the one who died. Raymond thought of seeing only the black light and waiting for the little flickers to disappear. Waiting for the bell to ring so he knew they were into the next round. Boxing, the way he knew it, didn't do the kind of good that he saw happen every day at the salon.

When one of the girls who worked at the shop suddenly quit on his sister because of a bad cough that wasn't going away, Raymond was given his own station. The first thing he did was put the plastic basket of supplies and lotions to the left of him. His sister didn't like that. "What the fuck, Raymond. You going southpaw on me now. You a right-hand. All your supplies go on the right. Fuck! Maybe you shoulda thought of that when you were boxing. You know how fucking hard southpaws are to fight—they do everything backwards. It's too late, isn't it. To go southpaw now."

Raymond didn't say anything. He just moved the basket to his right. He didn't like arguing or talking back to his sister. She'd always taken care of things, and of him. She talked tough and was for real tough, but she had a good heart. It was possible to be both.

His sister had him practise on a plastic hand. Thing was, it wasn't attached to anything. It was severed at the wrist and stood straight up in the air like it was waiting to give you a high-five. The plastic hand could be moved around for a better angle to paint a heart or put on dots. His sister watched him without saying a word. When he was done, she picked up the plastic hand and waved it in his face and said, "But hands come with fucking bodies! You can't be turning a client's hand three hundred and sixty degrees to draw a fucking heart! And is that what this is supposed to be, Raymond—a fucking heart? Looks to me like a stinking blob of disgusting shit."

She plopped the plastic hand down onto the empty station behind her, clearing Raymond's small surface area for him, and then held out her own hands. "Here," she said. "Try on me." For someone who did manicures all the time for other people, his sister sure didn't have the best nails. They were too long and yellowed at the tips, and her skin was dry and flaking. "Watch your fucking face! I know what you're thinking about these nails. If I paint them, the polish remover I use on clients will just fuck them up. And I ain't going to use that gel shit on myself. It's fucking expensive." He had started to cut her nails when she added, "Talk to me like I'm a client. Go on. Ask about my day, the weather, say something nice about me, try to make conversation." Raymond tried to think of what he could say, but before he could open his mouth his sister reassured him, "Don't you worry too much about this part. Most of the time they won't talk to you because they think you don't know how to speak English, which is fine because it's exhausting to make conversation. I don't care about their kids or husbands or boyfriends or what the fuck they're doing this week-end. If you don't want to talk to a client because you're tired or not interested, just turn to me and speak Lao. They'll think we're talking about them and that'll shut them right the fuck up."

For cheap nails, Raymond thought, he had to do and remember so much.

RAYMOND MADE A LOT of mistakes on the job. He would forget to brush off the excess nail polish on the bottle's mouth, so the polish went on too thick. He would check too soon to see if the paint was dry, pressing a finger on a client's painted nail and leaving a fingerprint. He also didn't leave enough room between the nail and the cuticle to draw out the shape of the nail. He had to start all over again each time, and what was supposed to be a twenty-minute job often took him an hour. But the clients his sister gave him were patient, and they didn't say anything about the hearts he drew even though they did appear to be, like his sister said, blobs of shit. No one complained. When they left, his sister said, "You see that, Raymond? I woulda been cussed out if I did what you did. But you? It's 'Oh sweetie, take your time' and 'Don't worry about it, honey. You're doing fine.'" Whenever his sister pretended to speak in the voice of a client, it was high-pitched and annoying, and she'd stand with one hand on her waist and float her other arm around and swat at the air. He had to admit, it was fun to work with her. She always found a way to make him laugh.

Over time, the work got easier. There was a pattern to the day and he just had to follow it. His sister liked to brag that Raymond was a boxer, and the clients seemed to like that this big, burly former fighter was handling their small hands. He thought some might be uncomfortable with a man handling them this way, but his sister told him the clients thought it was wonderful to be touched by that kind of muscle so gently.

Raymond was good with the endless repetition and with assessing what needed to be done. It reminded him of sparring at the gym, having to think and act quickly, anticipate what was coming, and then respond. Every client wanted something different, but there were some basic things everyone needed. He removed polish, cut nails, applied cuticle oil, and pushed skin away from the nails to give them a clean look and shape. Some nails had no shape; they came out straight and flat on the nail bed and he had to round them with a file. He had to work the file at a forty-five-degree angle, deciding where the nail should begin to bend. It was very subtle, the bend. At first, he wore a mask over his nose and mouth and he wore gloves too, but he couldn't get a proper grip and his clients couldn't hear what he said. After a few days he stopped wearing them, exposing himself to those tiny shards of nail dust that now entered and scratched at his lungs.

There were many nail polish colours. He couldn't remember them all so he just told his clients to pick a colour once they walked through the door: Shrimp Sunday Orange, Funny Cool Purple, Double Personality Blue, Alter Ego Pink. The names and colours went all along and around the walls. Because it was so unusual to see a man doing nails, or simply because they enjoyed a good flirting, his clients gave him twenty- or thirty-dollar tips. They told him, "Why don't you buy something nice for your little lady," or "Go out and have yourself a little fun, why don't you." His sister, always one to notice things, said, "Fuck! I'm lucky if I get two or three dollars. It's because you're a fucking man, isn't it? Even in a business I own myself and built up myself, men are still being paid more. And these are women who are doing this. They should know better!" And she'd look on angrily while he counted his tips, which often added up to more than what his sister charged for mani-pedis.

————

IF THERE WAS ONE THING that Raymond didn't like about the job, it was toes. After only a few weeks of working on them, he got warts on his hands.

His sister said, "Gross! I ain't gonna let anyone see that nasty shit while you're working on them! You better take time off. Plus, it might be contagious, I don't fucking know. I told you to wear gloves!"

He picked at a wart on his hand and winced.

His sister said, "You ain't gonna quit on me now because of this, are you? You know people come in just to see you. Never seen anything like that."

But it wasn't the warts he was worried about. Warts were nothing compared to how bad things could get in boxing, with the bad headaches and black lights and mumbling nonsense or being dead. Warts went away eventually. That didn't bother him. It was the smell of feet. It got into the pores of his nostrils and took root there, like a follicle of hair. It was becoming a part of him, the smell—like spoiled milk. He could never forget what he did for a living because it was always there. He was beginning to taste the smell of feet at the back of his throat. Soon he stopped enjoying food altogether, which made him lose weight, but his sister said this was a good thing since it meant more clients coming in to see him. She bought him tight-fitting black T-shirts and insisted he wear them at the shop. His muscles bulged out from the sleeves and the neck, the fabric clinging to him like an overstuffed sausage casing. His sister said, "Work it, Raymond. You don't got to be shy about what you got. Tighten it up, flex. We need that for the shop. It can't just be about the nails—anyone around here can do that."

Raymond was sure the warts did not come from his female clients. Most women took care of themselves. Their toes were clean and groomed to begin with, after years of salon and spa visits. He blamed the men. It was the men who had never had a pedicure their whole lives and wore heavy socks and leather boots all year round. The men who had been too embarrassed to show their untreated toes to a female pedicurist. Now that there was a man working at the salon, they came to him. As a man, Raymond knew not to mention or acknowledge the mess, the years of neglect just because the feet had been out of sight. The layers of skin he had to slough off like cutting a pat of butter. His sister would say, "You know why the skin there is yellow? Well, the fucking guy pees in the shower! That's why. Disgusting fucker!"

Still, Raymond didn't spend much time focusing on that part of the job.

Raymond had a favourite client. Miss Emily. He didn't have much to do when she came in. Her cuticles were already peeled back and her nail bed was long and thin and smooth. The skin on her hands and feet felt like a baby's, plump and soft. She would always do him the courtesy of removing her nail polish before she came in so he could start right away on the filing and paraffin wax, and then lay down the three layers of polish. The first layer was to protect the nail from the polish, the second layer was the polish colour itself, and the last layer was to help protect the polish from chipping and to keep it shiny.

At the start of each shift, Raymond would check the appointment log at the front desk, running his finger down all the names. When he saw that Miss Emily would be coming in, he would take a deep breath, as if some wonderful event was about to happen. He'd spend extra time polishing his tools and fluffing the chair's pillow. He even went out to buy a few red roses to put in a vase at his station. And after Miss Emily left, he couldn't stop smiling and asking the girl at the front desk when Miss Emily might come back to see him again.

One day his sister said, "What, you think you got a chance with that Miss Emily there? She's rich and educated. None of the things we are or are ever gonna be. Don't you be dreaming big now, little brother. Keep your dreams small. The size of a grain of rice. And cook that shit up and swallow it every night, then shit that fucking thing out in the morning. It ain't ever gonna happen. If there's something I know in this life, it's rich women. And that woman ain't for you." But even when his sister talked him down like that, Raymond just kept daydreaming about Miss Emily. When she didn't come in, he painted and shaped all his clients' nails like Miss Emily's. Anyone could be her.

Then one afternoon, while he was sweeping the floor by the glass door, he looked up and saw Miss Emily with a man. Raymond watched the two of them, standing close together, touching hands. He hadn't seen anyone with her before. The man wore a three-piece suit and expensive shoes. The black leather had a polished shine to it, and where his toes bent there wasn't a crease. Raymond put the broom away and sat down at his station to prepare. When Miss Emily came in and took the seat, the smell of this man's cologne came in with her. It was not one of those drugstore scents. Raymond knew about those. He had tried them all. Although Raymond held Miss Emily's hand over his small work station, he felt a wide space between them. Her smile was just polite, and nothing more. His sister had been watching him and she saw his face fall, the way it would fall in the ring when he knew he was losing.

Later, Raymond's sister drove him home. It was their routine, and the one moment of the day when they could be brother and sister—a family again. Raymond didn't get out of the car right away. He didn't want to go in to his apartment just yet. The sun was out and he wanted to feel it on his face.

As they sat in the car outside his apartment, his sister lit up a cigarette and smoked with the windows rolled down. She shook her head. "Raymond. Didn't I tell you. You've got to not have dreams. That woman ain't ever gonna love a man who does nails. That's not real life. You and me here, we live in the real world. You're given a place and you just do your best in it. Fucking give it up.

I hate when you get like this. Plenty of girls for you! They want to get with you all the time, but you don't let yourself see it. Like the girls at the shop. They're all wet for you."

Those girls were married or serious with someone. What his sister didn't know was what they talked about behind her back when she went out for a smoke or to go get supplies. How they tried to get pregnant, but no babies ever caught on because of the chemicals from the salon. How their coughs started and didn't ever stop. How they wanted to quit but had nowhere else to go.

Raymond didn't like to talk back to his sister, but this time he thought she was wrong to say what she did. "Well," he said, "you know, maybe Miss Emily ain't ever gonna be with a man like me, but I want to dream it anyway. It's a nice feeling and I ain't had one of those things to myself in a long time. I know I don't got a chance in hell, but it's something to get me through. It's to get through the next hour, the next day. Don't you go reminding me what dreams a man like me ought to have. That I can dream at all means something to me."

Raymond's sister didn't say anything. She just stared straight ahead beyond the steering wheel. He knew his face resembled hers, but damaged—a dented nose, the left eyebrow split and made crooked by a scar. Although her face was treated to facials and creams and anti-wrinkle serums and was smooth and glowing, Raymond could tell she felt the way his face looked, beaten and busted. She didn't want to recognize that face and see it hoping. Hope was a terrible thing for her—it meant it wasn't there for you, whatever it was you were hoping for.

After a moment, she went back to her cigarette. Every puff was a small grey cloud that disappeared like the dreams she was always telling him to keep small. Raymond dropped his head and gazed down at his palms, where the warts that would put him out of work for a few more weeks were coming in again.

They sat there in silence, in the oncoming darkness, the car windows still open. They could hear a family in their backyard somewhere nearby, the sizzle on the barbecue, and the giggling—young and fragile and innocent. It was the kind of giggling they themselves did as kids. Now, that kind of giggle seemed foolish for them to do. It was like a far distant thing, a thing that happened only to other people. All they could do now was be close to it, and remain out of sight.

Chick-A-Chee!

OUR BUILDING HAD FIVE FLOORS, and each one looked the same—two green doors on one side of a hallway facing two green doors on the other side. We didn't know anyone else who lived in the building. We kept to ourselves and didn't walk around on the other floors. There was no reason to—you only went to the door where you lived.

My brother and I were often left at home alone after school, even though he was six and I was only seven. Dad worked at a factory putting wires into electrical cords, and if he didn't reach his target numbers for the day, he'd sometimes have to work the night shift to get it done. Most of the time he worked twelve-hour days, taking his lunch break around four in the afternoon so he could pick us up from school and drop us off at home before going back to work. Mom couldn't leave work to do anything like that because we only had one car and Dad drove it.

Every time Dad left us to go back to work, he'd remind me to put the chain on the door and to keep quiet, and not to open the door for anyone, not even if they said they were a friend. He had me go over the places in the apartment where we could hide if we got scared: under the bed, in the bathtub behind the shower curtain, in the shoe closet.

If we were ever in trouble, Dad said, we were not to go to the neighbours for help, or to call 9-1-1. He said it would be like calling the cops on him—he would be the one who'd get in trouble for leaving us alone and unsupervised. Whatever trouble we were in, we would have to handle it ourselves, he said. Then he'd point to where he kept a small red axe with a wooden handle hidden behind the radiator.

The first time he put the axe in my hand, the handle was surprisingly light. Dad said, "Now, you only get one chance, so go for the neck or the face. Right here"—he pointed to the left side of his neck—"is where you should aim for." I lifted the axe up high, but Dad chuckled and said the blade was turned the other way. He came over and showed me how the sharp end is the part that does the damage. I raised the axe over my head again and then brought it down in a single chop. This time, Dad laughed as though he was just watching me throw a rubber ball— a laugh that said it was cute, what I was doing. When he saw how nervous I was, he said, "Ah, don't worry. I've done worse things than this at your age. Younger even, maybe." Dad reassured me that I'd probably never have to use the axe, but it was important for me to know I could.

But all I could think of was the time when, late at night, someone came to our door and banged on it loudly, yelling, "Open the door! I've got a knife!" Me and my brother stood by the door, terrified, and thought of the places we could go hide while Dad went to peer through the peephole. When the banging wouldn't stop, we held on to our father, each grabbing fistfuls of his shirt. I was so relieved we weren't alone, and that it was a Sunday and Dad wasn't working an extra shift at the factory but was home with us. Dad looked down at the both of us and brought a finger up to his lips so we wouldn't say anything. Then he whispered that he had been thinking of opening the door but changed his mind after the man said he had a knife. "That's no way to ask anyone for help!" Dad laughed and slapped his knee, and my brother and I laughed too, but quietly, so that the man on the other side of the door wouldn't hear us.

The next morning, as we left for school, I noticed there was a smear of blood on our door.

MOST SATURDAYS, DAD drove us all out to a neighbour-hood we wished we could live in, with wide, tree-lined roads and big Victorian homes. It was something we did on our way to Chinatown to buy groceries. We would drive slowly down the street, pick which house we wanted to live in, and point to the window where we wanted our bedrooms to be. My parents and my brother always chose the large, sprawling houses, but I paid attention to the things people left outside. Sometimes there were hockey sticks, unmarked goalie pads, and a net left out in the driveway, or a pink bike abandoned on the front lawn. It seemed to me no one here was ever afraid someone would take their stuff if they could just leave it all lying out in the open like that, not put away or locked up with a chain.

One time, I noticed that every house on that street had raw pumpkins on their front steps—either a giant one or a cluster of little ones. There were faces carved into most of them: triangle eyes, a circle for the nose, and a mouth with one or two teeth hanging from inside a wide smile. A few of them had the seeds pulled out and arranged around the pumpkin's mouth as if it were throwing up. At school, we had painted orange circles or cut them out of orange cardboard paper and glued googly eyes on them.

I leaned forward from the back seat and asked Dad, "How come people here love pumpkins so much?" and he said, "Humph. Seems like a waste of food to me." After we looked at all those pumpkins, Dad said to Mom, "No one would put poison or sharp blades in their candy in a neighbourhood like this, would they." Then he turned back to us and yelled, "I've got a knife! Open the door!" And me and my brother screamed like we were scared, but we were not at all.

After that, in October of every year until my brother turned nine, our parents always took us out to "Chick-A-Chee."

The first time we went, my brother put a white bed-sheet over his head, with holes cut out for his eyes and for his arms. Dad didn't have much time to make him anything. He had spent weeks making me a tight-fitting long-sleeved black shirt and matching pants with glow-in-the-dark fabric bones sewn on in the front. In the dark, you wouldn't see me at all. You would just see a skeleton walking across the room. It made my brother squeal with excitement, knowing that someday soon this outfit would be passed on to him like everything else I'd ever had.

It was unusual to see Dad come home from work so early. I didn't understand why, and worried he'd lost his job. It was something he always told us, that he had to work long hours or he wouldn't have a job at all. But then he told us to put our costumes on and he drove us out to that neighbourhood we wanted to live in, even though we weren't buying groceries. Dad parked the car and told us we were to walk from house to house dressed like this, then yell "Chick-A-Chee!" at the person who answered the door and hold out our open pillowcases for them to fill with all kinds of candies. I did not believe him. I was certain then that he really had lost his job and what we were doing was part of his plan to send us away, something our parents often threatened when we were misbehaving or we wanted something they didn't have the money for. I wanted to cry, but I saw how my brother was looking at me—like he needed me to be brave for the both of us.

Dad got out of the car and tilted the seat forward so my brother and I could get out. He took us both by the hand and led us to the first house. It was huge, the windows as large as doors, and I wondered who lived here. As my brother and I climbed up the front steps alone, we turned around to make sure Dad was still there. He was standing by the curb, hands in his pockets, only pulling them out to puff warm air into them. He was dressed in a light jacket and jeans, his idea of looking good. A warm coat and mittens would cramp his style. When he noticed us still standing on the steps, just looking at him, he encouraged us to go on, lifting both arms and sweeping the air in front of him, reminding us, "Say Chick-A-Chee!"

When we got to the door, we stood there trying to find the doorbell like Dad had told us to do. "That's how you know it's a nice house," he had said. "It's so big, no one inside would hear a knock at the front door, so you have to push a button to ring a bell."

My brother tapped my arm and pointed to the button on the right side of the door. It turned out that neither of us could reach it. I lifted my brother up and he pressed the doorbell once, and again, and then I let him down softly. A light came on and a woman with brown, shoulder-length hair and blunt bangs opened the door. She wore glasses and had a friendly smile. She said, "Well, now, you are a ghost . . . and you are . . . oh my! Look at that costume! Now, isn't that a sight! Where did you get that? Did your mother make it?"

I was too nervous to answer her, so I whispered, "Chick-A-Chee."

"Oh, Harold, come out here! These children are just so adorable! Harooooold! Get out here!"

Harold came to the door, shuffling his fluffy slippers along the floor.

"Chick-A-Chee," I said again softly.

Harold gave a laugh and said, "Elaaaaine! That is so adoooorable! Give the kids a little extra, won't you?" And he reached for a large glass bowl from somewhere behind the door and dropped two bags of potato chips in each pillowcase.

As soon as the treats were in our pillowcases, we both shouted, "Chick-A-Chee!" and ran away from the house, giggling like we'd gotten away with something we never thought we could have. We ran to Dad, who was still standing by the curb, and showed him the potato chip bags at the bottom of the pillowcases.

"See! I told you," he said. "Just say Chick-A-Chee!"

And all through the night, we went from door to door yelling "Chick-A-Chee!" until our pillowcases were so heavy we couldn't carry them anymore. There were other children in the neighbourhood dressed up as princesses, pumpkins, witches, and baseball players. We didn't know any of them. Sometimes, we would end up on the same front porch with a group of them, and we would hold out our pillowcases and they would hold out plastic pumpkins with handles. When my brother and I said, "Chick-A-Chee!" the people behind the door always told us to come closer so they could give us more candy.

When we got home, Dad and Mom emptied the pillowcases and sorted the candy. We couldn't have anything homemade, or any loosely wrapped or already-opened things.

At school the next day, my brother and I took out our candies at lunch and displayed them on a table like we were street vendors, telling our friends we went Chick-A-Chee where the houses were gigantic. Our friends had kept to their buildings or to the houses next door or hadn't gone out at all, so they had only little gum balls or one or two tiny chocolate bars. We had bags and bags of chips, whole chocolate bars, and packs of gum—and there was more waiting for us at home.

The lunch woman on duty leaned through the crowd around us and said, "Don't you mean you went trick-or-treating?"

We shook our heads. The woman did not know what she was talking about. I looked up at her big, round, intrusive face and said, "No, Missus Furman. We went Chick-A-Chee!"

The Universe Would Be So Cruel

MR. VONG STRETCHED his neck to peer over the heads of the wedding guests, trying to get a good view of the bride and groom. When he spotted them, he turned to his wife and daughter and made a bold prediction: "Ah, don't they look lovely. Too bad it isn't going to last."

Mr. Vong had been invited not because he was a relative or because he was a friend of the family. The young couple had turned to him because he was the only printer in town who offered Lao lettering on wedding invitations. He was highly sought-after for his Lao fonts, his eloquence with the language, his knowledge of how little things can shape big outcomes. Sure, his clients could download the fonts themselves and print them out at Kinko's, but that kind of lazy effort might signify a lazy marriage, one where their bond might break at the first sign of trouble.

Mr. Vong printed other things at his shop besides wedding invitations. He didn't make much money. Most of his clients were the ones the bigger printers didn't want to deal with—men and women who worked for themselves, who didn't buy in bulk, who didn't have time to be on the Internet, and who didn't speak English (through hand signals and sounds, Mr. Vong found a way to communicate with them). He liked these clients best. The farmers with dirt under their fingernails from working out on the fields all day, the butchers who didn't have time to change out of clothes stained with blood, the seamstresses who only had twenty minutes before they had to get back to work. They reminded him of himself—all of them doing the grunt work of the world.

The clients he didn't like were the salesmen who came in wearing expensive business suits yet always asked him to give them a deal. He recognized them by the sheen of the watches on their wrists, their slicked-back hair and warm-weather tans, their perfect English. The way they looked at him like he was going to be some joke they'd tell a friend about later, calling him "buddy," correcting his spelling. He always chased these men away with a "Fuck you!" Sometimes, when he was in a good mood and had time to spare, he would humour them, allow them in his shop for fifteen minutes, let them talk on and on and show him their graphs of sales and profits—some fancy business-school way of doing things. But eventually, he'd get around to yelling at them like he did the others who had come before. Those men were protected by their glass office towers and their secretaries and lawyers and cheating tax accountants, but in his shop, one he owned and operated alone, he was boss! To own a thing yourself, and to be able to say, "Fuck you! All of you all! Fuck you into hell!" It had been something that was said to him and it was fun to turn the tables and say it to someone else, to see them lose their cool and make a quick, fumbling exit.

Of all the things Mr. Vong made and printed at the shop, though, it was Lao wedding invitations that gave him the most joy. Mr. Vong took great care with his invitations. He made his own paper, every fibre dried and flattened in his shop, the process taking several months. He even mixed his own pigment, creating a final shade that was unique. He kept a record of all the colours and shades he had used in a scrapbook, little tiny squares with the names and date of each one. To use the same colour pigment more than once might invite the idea that no marriage was unique. He wore a headpiece with jeweller's magnifying glasses attached and went over every single letter on the invitations. He was determined to get the smallest of details exactly right—a spelling error could be a sign that the couple was not perfect for each other. He was the guardian of their good fortune. And he was the best.

The engaged couple was very pleased with Mr. Vong's care and expertise. When they saw the Lao language on their wedding invitations, its loops and swirls, its curlicues like ribbons, the couple squealed and said, "Oh Mr. Vong! Mr. Vong! We love these. They're perfect. So beautiful. What are you doing in June? You must come to the wedding. You must! We couldn't have done this without you." The both of them grinning wide with their blindingly bright, even teeth.

IT WAS WHILE the bride and groom were having their first dance as husband and wife that Mr. Vong made his bold prediction.

"Just you mark my words," Mr. Vong continued. "The marriage will last less than a year. "

"Ai, why are you saying this for?" Mrs. Vong said. "Keep your voice down!" she urged, slapping him on his arm and glancing around at the people seated at their table to see if they had heard. But everyone was paying attention to the bride and groom, some reaching for their spouse's hand, musing over their own first dance in front of family and friends, or eating the food on their plates so they could go and get seconds. The guests had just been served a nice meal of papaya salad, spring rolls, sticky rice, minced chicken with fresh herbs and spices, and sweets wrapped in banana leaves.

"Less than a year. That's my prediction. And you know I'm always right about these things. You know," he said, pointing to his twenty-seven-year-old daughter.

She nodded her head in agreement, and he went on. "If I paid for a whole lobster, I'm going to get it." He was referring to how whenever they ordered a lobster dinner—the most expensive thing on the menu—Mr. Vong just had to make sure that he got what he paid for. The lobster shells might have been cracked open or chewed to a pulp, but he told everyone to put the shells back onto the main plate so he could rearrange the broken bits, unfold the bones to their original shape, and reassemble the lobster's body back together to see if there was something missing. Once, there was one claw, half a tail, and some legs missing. Mr. Vong knew it! He called the waiter over, made a big show out of being cheated, and made sure the whole restaurant knew *he* was not one to tolerate such a cheat.

"I know. I know these things," he said. Then he returned to his meal, gathering up the minced chicken with a flattened ball of sticky rice.

True enough, in less than a year the bride and groom were divorced.

LATER THAT YEAR, Mr. Vong made another one of his predictions. This time he made it the minute he opened the wedding invitation. He said, "Ah, not even going to happen."

"Dad, what is it? How can you know it's not going to happen?"

"Look at it. The invitation was printed at some fancy downtown place."

"Yeah. So?"

"So, they don't do Lao lettering at that place. Look at that," he said, pointing to the text of the invitation, "it's all in English."

"Maybe the bride and groom don't read Lao."

"It doesn't matter! The language should be there whether you can read it or not. It's where you come from. Why leave it out?"

His daughter came over to look at the invitation. There was no Lao lettering to be found anywhere on this particular invitation. It was fancy—thick paper and raised print she could feel when she ran a hand across the lettering, the little silver-glinted bumps forming the names, addresses, dates. And yes, Mr. Vong's prediction was correct. The would-be groom broke off the engagement to marry someone *else* named Sue. Phone calls were made. The wedding was cancelled. Called off.

"Dad, seriously, *how did you know?*"

"Look, I know these things. You just can't have a Lao wedding without Lao letters on the invitation. And you have to have your real given name on there. Yeah, it's a long name—but that's *your* name. Why would you want to be Sue when your name is really Savongnavathakad? Because, you know, the real Sue will end up marrying the guy if it says so right there on the invitation."

———

WHEN IT WAS TIME for Mr. Vong's daughter to get married, he spared no expense. He ordered sparkled paint from Laos made out of the crushed wings of a rare local insect. The gold specks were real and not artificial—real shine and shimmer for a real marriage. He printed the invitations by hand and left each one out to dry on a metal rack. Ten on each rack for a total of two hundred invitations, an even number, always divisible by two—an important number in a marriage. Mr. Vong didn't use a fan to dry the paint because he wanted them to dry on their own. What might have taken only a few hours instead took four days. It was his opinion that using a machine was cheating. He did everything he could possibly do to ensure that his daughter's wedding invitations were perfect and ready to be sent out into the scrutiny of the universe.

On the day of the wedding, Mr. Vong's daughter wore a sleeveless white wedding dress. It was plain, without lace or buttons, but the fabric cascaded down her body like a fountain of milk.

But the groom was not there. Jilted.

When it became clear the groom was not coming, Mr. Vong's daughter lifted up the bottom of her dress and ran over to him, furious. "It's all your fault, isn't it? The invitations. Something must have gone wrong!"

Mr. Vong tried to think of an answer, one he could use to explain how the wedding had come to this. "I . . . I found one invitation behind the door," he said. "I must have missed it. All invitations must go out at the same time. It was just the one. I didn't know the universe would be so cruel. I am sorry."

It was not true, of course. Not even close. He had accounted for everything! And now, no amount of fuck-you-to-hells could make a difference to that boy. But how could he tell her that the boy she loved wasn't kind or good, that he didn't love her, that sometimes what felt like love only *felt* like love and wasn't real. He couldn't do anything about that but say, "Yes, yes, it was my fault. It is all my fault."

Edge of the World

WHEN I WAS ABOUT FOUR, my mother and I spent our days sitting side by side on the couch, watching soap operas and eating chocolates and laughing. My mother's laugh was loud and wild. She never covered her mouth, which would open so wide I could see the half-chewed chocolate mashed up against the inside of her cheek. She would only laugh this way when we were alone. With my father or in the company of others, she would giggle and put a hand over her mouth. I wanted everyone to see what I saw when we were alone.

My mother learned to speak English watching these soaps, and soon she started practising what she learned. When my father didn't feel like eating, she would ask who he had been eating his meals with that he had no appetite? When a sock went missing from the dryer, she would ask where it went, and when he had no answer, she would accuse him of having an affair.

My father didn't take my mother seriously. He tried to keep their talk light, saying he sure wished he wasn't so busy working and that life really was as full of opportunities for affairs as she imagined it to be. But he would turn serious afterwards, saying, "You don't know, do you. What it's like for me at work. They all talk so fast in English. Barking at me all the time about keeping up. Sometimes I don't even feel like a human being."

My parents didn't spend much time alone, and when they did, there were no Lao bars or cafés or restaurants for them to go out to. Occasionally, we were invited over to get-togethers at the homes of other Lao refugees. There were those who had been here a long time, like us, and there were those who had just arrived. These parties were where everyone went to dance and listen to music, play cards and eat, reminisce and talk about old times. They would laugh all night—sad, faint bursts of air—and shake their heads in disbelief at what they had made of themselves in this new country.

My parents went to these parties to hear the news from back home or to ask what had happened to those they left behind. Who was still there? Was their house still standing? And if they made it out of Laos, which refugee camp did they end up in? How long were they there? And where did they land? When my parents read the newspaper or watched the evening news, they never heard anything about what was happening in their country. It was almost as if it didn't exist.

My father was often at the centre of these parties. A wave of laughter would crash in from the living room and when I peered inside he would be there, telling everyone his stories. The one everyone seemed to love to hear him tell was the "Yes, sir" story, and even though they had all heard it before, he would begin the story as if they hadn't. He told them how he said "Yes, sir!" in English at work whenever anyone told him what to do, but he said it with the tone and force of a "Fuck you!" Then he marched around the room and saluted everyone like a dutiful soldier, saying in English, "Yes, *sir*! Yes, *sir*! Yes, *sir*!" each time. He cackled with glee at how the people at work thought he was so polite and nice.

My mother watched and listened to all of this from the kitchen, but she never joined in. She kept to herself, eating a plate of food while surrounded by Tupperware, glass casserole dishes, steaming pots, simmering pans, plastic forks and spoons and paper plates. I stayed there with her, and she told me what each dish was and how it was supposed to be cooked. She pointed out that some of the key ingredients were missing and said that none of the dishes could live up to her memory of the real thing. She said the food in Laos just tasted better and that maybe someday when I was older we could go back and visit. She said all this to me in Lao.

A woman in the kitchen overheard her and said, "Your child understands Lao?" My mother was proud that I could still have something from the old country even though I had never been there. But the woman said to her, "Oh no, no! Oy! You better start speaking English with her. How's she going to fit in once she gets to school?!" When the woman left the kitchen, we laughed at her, how worried sick she seemed about not fitting in with everybody, as if that was a thing to want.

Later, my mother encouraged me to go and play with the other kids at the party. They were rowdy and running around and speaking English with one another. I wanted to play with them, but they kept pushing me on the arm and telling me I was "it." I did not know what "it" was, but every time I tried to get near one of them, any time I came close, they'd run from me like they didn't want to play with me at all. After a while I went back to the kitchen, and when my mother saw me return she asked what had happened, why I came back so soon. I told her, "All they do is speak English. I don't know what they're playing." Then she paused a moment and said, "Maybe it's something they learned at school. You'll learn too, when you go."

The closest my mother came to having friends were the cashiers at the Goodwill. They were friendly and knew her by name, and they'd let her wander the aisles there for hours. They might only have been doing their jobs, but my mother didn't see it that way. Once, she brought them egg rolls wrapped in aluminum foil, and they took them to the backroom to eat while we picked through the clothing together. But the way my mother walked by the racks, with a hand trailing behind her, it was as if she wasn't really looking for anything she wanted. It made me wonder if she might have wanted to be invited to the backroom to enjoy the food. To distract her from thinking about her egg rolls, I grabbed a yellow dress and brought it to her. I said, "What do you think of this colour?" She looked at the price tag—one dollar—and nodded. Before we left the store, my mother glanced back at the cashiers. She said to me, "You think they liked it?"

ONCE I STARTED SCHOOL, my mother watched the soaps alone and told me about them when I came home. There was always an affair, a long-lost twin, someone in a coma, a handsome doctor. After a while, I didn't want to hear about them anymore. I started reading books, and my mother would come sit with me and have me read them to her. She would ask questions about the drawings inside. The books she liked best were the scratch-and-sniff ones, and the ones where animals popped out at you. Each time I pulled the paper tab and a cat or a dog jumped out, she would draw in her breath, surprised and delighted by such a thing. There was one book about a sheep, with a cotton patch inside. My mother would pet the cotton with her finger as if it was alive.

At night, she would bring a book to my bed and insist I read it to her. There were not too many words inside.

Sometimes she'd fall asleep right away, but when she didn't, I would make up stories for her. "No one is ever alone in the world," I said. "There is always a friend somewhere for everyone." She must have been twenty-four then, but she seemed much younger—and smaller. I watched over her, and when she shivered I pulled a blanket up to cover her, trying not to wake her. Sometimes she had nightmares. I could tell by how she was breathing—short, panicked breaths. I would reach out and stroke her hair, tell her things would be all right, though I didn't know if they would be or what it meant to say those words. I just knew it helped to say them.

I never thought to ask my mother why she slept in my room most nights. I was just glad not to be alone in the dark.

ONE SATURDAY MORNING, we wandered into the toy section of the Goodwill, and my mother picked something out for me. It was a map of the world, a puzzle, a thousand cardboard pieces inside a paper box for fifty cents. Each piece had a unique shape that fit into another. The point was to find the other pieces that fit into it somewhere in this pile of shapes and lock them together.

When we got home and I sat down to work on the puzzle, she did not pick up a piece or try to help me put it together. Instead, she watched me and what I did. She'd say, "That one doesn't go there. Try another one."

When one fit, she'd say, "Every piece belongs somewhere, doesn't it."

I worked on the puzzle when I came home from school, and piece by piece, I put the colours together. First the blues, which stood for the oceans. Then the reds, greens, oranges, yellows, and pinks of all the many different countries. Weeks later, there were only a handful of pieces left, and when I put in the last piece, I announced, with pride, "Ma, I'm finished!"

My mother peered at the puzzle and pointed at a green spot, said that was where she was from. A tiny country on the lower far right. Then she pointed to where we were at this moment, a large pink area at the top far left. After a moment, she pointed to the puzzle's edge and then to the floor, where there was nothing. "It's dangerous there," she said. "You fall off."

"No, you don't," I said. "The world is round. It's like a ball."

But my mother insisted, "That's not right."

Still, I continued, "When you get to the edge you just come right back around to the other side."

"How do you know?" she asked.

"My teacher says. Miss Soo says." There was a globe on Miss Soo's desk at school, and whenever she talked about the oceans or the continents or plate tectonics, she would point to those features on it. I didn't know if what Miss Soo was telling me was true. I hadn't thought to ask.

"It's flat," my mother said, touching the map. "Like this." Then she swept the puzzle to the floor with her palm. All the connected pieces broke off from each other, the hours lost in a single gesture. "Just because I never went to school doesn't mean I don't know things."

I thought of what my mother knew then. She knew about war, what it felt like to be shot at in the dark, what death looked like up close in your arms, what a bomb could destroy. Those were things I didn't know about, and it was all right not to know them, living where we did now, in a country where nothing like that happened. There was a lot I did not know.

We were different people, and we understood that then.

A FEW WEEKS AFTER, we went to the park. It was cold and the grass was yellow underneath a lumpy sheet of ice. Earlier, I had been reading and my mother had been watching television. She usually found a show to make her laugh, but that day she couldn't settle on one. She kept pressing the button on the remote control, flipping to the next channel, and then the next, until she started all over again.

I rushed over to the swings, hopped on the seat of one, and pumped my legs so I shot myself high into the air. My mother sat on a park bench alone, in her blue winter coat, facing me. She was not far. I called to her to pay attention to me, to see how high I was going all by myself, but her head was turned away, her eyes focused on something else.

I stopped swinging and turned to see what she was looking at, the swing slowly coming to a halt. A man had run out of an apartment building in his boxers and a white T-shirt. He seemed flustered, in a hurry, as though he had not planned to be outside in the cold dressed like that.

A woman dressed in a pantsuit had followed him out. Heels tapping on the sidewalk like a pencil on a table.

The man glanced behind him, stopped, and screamed, "It's over. We're finished!" When the woman tried to embrace him, he refused, batting away her arms.

I walked over to where my mother was and stood right in front of her, blocking her view of the couple. I said, "Let's go home." She looked up at me and there were tears in her eyes. "It's snowing," she said and glanced away. She said it once, like that. In a small clear voice. *It's snowing.* But the way she said it made it seem like it was not about snow at all. Something that I can't ever know about her. Then my mother looked up at me again and said, "I never have to worry about you, do I." I nodded, even though I wasn't sure if it was really a question.

Soon after, sometime in the night when I was asleep, she walked out the door with a suitcase. My father saw her leave, he told me. And he did nothing.

———

ALL THIS WAS YEARS AGO, but I can still feel the sadness of that time, waiting for her to come back. I know now what I couldn't have known then—she wouldn't just be gone, she'd stay gone. I don't think about why she left. It doesn't matter anymore. What matters is that she did. What more is there to think about than that?

Often, I dream of seeing her face, still young like she was then, and although I can't remember the sound of my mother's voice, she is always trying to tell me something, her lips wrapped around shapes I can't hear. The dream might last only a few seconds, but that's all it takes, really, to undo the time that has passed and has been put between us. I wake from these dreams raw, a child still, though I am forty-five now, and grieve the loss of her again and again.

My father did not grieve. He had done all of this life's grieving when he became a refugee. To lose your love, to be abandoned by your wife was a thing of luxury even— it meant you were alive.

THE OTHER NIGHT, I saw an image of the Earth on the evening news. I had seen it many times before, and although my mother was not there, I spoke to her anyway as if she was. "See? It really is round. Now we know for sure." I said it out loud again, and even though it disappeared, I knew what I said had become a sound in the world.

Afterwards, I went to the bathroom mirror and stared at the back of my mouth. I opened my mouth wide, saw the hot, wet, pink flesh, and the dark centre where my voice came out of, and I laughed, loud and wild. The sound went into the air vent, and I imagined people living in the building wondering to themselves where a sound like that came from, what could make a woman laugh like that at this hour of the night.

The School Bus Driver

THE SCHOOL BUS DRIVER was named Jai. It rhymed with *chai*. He was looking at his wife's breasts in a photograph. They were tight and perky in the white spandex top she wore. Below that, her bikini bottom was just a patch of cloth in the front, held up by thin strings tied into a small bow. She was sitting on the white sheets of an unmade hotel bed and looking straight at the camera, her knees tucked underneath her. The school bus driver thought his wife looked odd in these vacation pictures. She'd never posed this way before, for him. Her black hair was set in big soft curls and she looked like a child's doll: blue eyelids, long artificial eyelashes, round rosy cheeks, red lips. She would never, on her own, make herself up like this. This bikini would never be something she'd choose for herself. "Hee keyow," she would say, shaking her head in disapproval if he ever suggested she wear anything even slightly revealing. This bikini must have been Frank's idea.

"Oh, Frank. He's such a goofball," she said, giggling, trying to make light of the whole thing. Frank was her boss at Coffee Time.

The school bus driver had intended the trip to Laos to be a surprise gift for his wife. She was working long hours these days; she deserved a nice vacation. He bought one plane ticket (it was all he could afford at the time), thinking she'd go alone to see her family. But when she asked Frank for time off from work, he said she could go—if he came along.

"I've always wanted to see a foreign country with a native," Frank had said.

He was in almost every one of these photos, smiling and posing with her cousins, parents, grandparents. But in the photos where Jai's wife was in the white bikini, it must have been Frank behind the camera. There were so many of her alone.

THE SCHOOL BUS DRIVER and his wife lived in a newly built brick house—two-car garage, four bedrooms, two bathrooms, and a finished basement. There were two other houses exactly like it on the block. The developer was supposed to tear down the neighbouring shopping mall and parking lot to build more new homes like theirs, but there was some problem with the fees, the licences, the zoning approvals—it got too messy for the builder to deal with. So now, there were just these three identical brick houses between a shopping mall parking lot and a tall apartment building, all facing a busy main street. The developer needed to unload these homes quick, so no one questioned whether the bus driver and his wife could really afford it. Still, they owned a home of their own now, even if they couldn't quite manage the mortgage payments. How could they, with the school bus driver working part-time and his wife making minimum wage at Coffee Time? They just barely made the monthly payments.

Sometimes when they were very short on money, the school bus driver's wife would come home with extra cash, saying that Frank had given her a bonus at work. She said it was a bonus for her good work. "Just this one time. This bonus. For my good work," she said. Frank was really good to them in that way.

SINCE HER TRIP to Laos with Frank, the school bus driver's wife had started to put in longer hours at work. She came home much later than usual now. At first, she blamed the bus schedule—they didn't come as frequently after dark. She said, "You don't know how scary it is, to be a woman standing there at the bus stop at night. I hold my keys in my hand and put them between my fingers so I'm ready to defend myself against some pervert. *You just don't know!*"

It didn't make sense to him, but she was right. He didn't know what it was like for a woman. The school bus driver suggested he pick her up after work. But she laughed and said, "Not in that big yellow thing you drive."

So she arranged for her friend Frank to pick her up on the way to work and to drive her home too. He was going to and leaving from the same place and at the same time, after all. It was only reasonable.

Frank drove a dark-green Jaguar. It was fancy. You never heard the engine at all, creeping down the street to pick up the school bus driver's wife or to drop her off after work. He took good care of this car. Even in the winter, when there was snow, Frank's car was always newly washed and polished. All year round, he kept it like this.

When the school bus driver thought about how things used to be, he would remember what his wife used to smell like when she first started working at Coffee Time, a bit like burnt coffee beans. He had to admit to himself that she seemed happier now, not having to rely on public transit. Now she smelled of cigars. Frank's cigars. The scent was a bit metallic and dusty. Frank probably smoked in the car. That's how the smell got all over her like that.

THE FIRST TIME it happened was on a Saturday afternoon. Frank came over. He rode up in his dark-green

Jaguar and parked it in their driveway as if he lived there now. The school bus driver thought it was odd for Frank to stop by on a weekend, when his wife didn't have to be at work. She greeted him at the door, invited him in. The school bus driver was watching television in the living room, but they did not join him.

His wife said they had to talk about work. "Very boring," she said.

They went into the bedroom.

The lock clicked into place.

He wondered what they were doing, if they were naked together. If so, how they kept it all so quiet. He didn't want to make a big deal of it.

"WHY DON'T YOU want me to have any friends!" his wife said when he asked her about what happened in the bedroom with Frank. He hated arguments. He would do anything to avoid them. He had thought of forgetting this whole thing, but he didn't want to be seen as spineless or, worse, not caring. Other times, when he tried to protest, to confront them, Frank would step in, his face red and sweaty, the white patches of his hair damp and rumpled, and say, "Be cool about this."

Sometimes he was certain Frank was mocking him, but it was just too awful to think about. How could he be sure, and to whom could he bring this up? His wife would just say he was jealous of their friendship, and accuse him again of not letting her have any friends. He didn't want to seem like a possessive, jealous husband, even if that's how he was feeling.

"Jay. People form this kind of friendship in this country," she said.

He thought for a few seconds that she was talking about someone else, or to someone else. But then he realized, that's what his name was now. Jay. Like blue jay, a small blue bird, a little dot in the sky. He wanted to remind his wife that his name was Jai. *It means* heart *in Lao!* he wanted to yell. But then she would just remind him how men in this country do not raise their voices at women. Or tell him to practise his English. "No one here knows *jai* means *heart*," she would say. So what if that's what it means? It doesn't mean anything in English. And English is the only language that matters here.

"That is just the way things are here," she said.

And if he was going to live here, he had to learn to adapt and fit in and not be so uptight.

"Be cool," she said in her perfect English, sounding just like Frank.

ON MONDAY MORNING, the school bus driver went to the parking lot to dig his bus out of the snow. He took the shovel he had bought from Canadian Tire and started shovelling around the wheels. It had snowed five inches overnight, but the snow was light and fluffy; it hadn't had time to harden or turn into ice yet. The shovelling was easy. In less than ten minutes he moved the snow out of the way as easily as if he were dusting. He did not really have to shovel the bus out—the tires could have handled it—but out of habit, he did.

He thought about clearing off the snow from the top of the bus. He didn't want the snow to fall off in chunks and land on a car driving behind him. But even with the shovel he couldn't reach the top of the bus on his own and he hadn't brought a ladder. For now, this would just have to do. When the school bus driver was done shovelling around the wheels, he threw the shovel on the floor of the front seat and turned on the engine to warm up the inside of the bus. From the driver's seat, he noticed a yellow slip of paper tucked underneath the windshield wiper.

Another one.

He went outside again, grabbed the parking ticket, and folded it until it became a tiny square. He tucked it into his wallet, underneath a picture of his wife. It was an old photo of her, in black and white, taken when they were still in Laos. She was smiling. Her hair was parted in the middle, her face plain, her smile shy. Next to the photo was a plastic flap that held his driver's licence. He looked at his first name. Jai. It rhymes with *chai*. It means heart. Heart.

You Are So Embarrassing

EVERYTHING OUTSIDE WAS BLURRY and wet, and there was nothing to be done about it. The windshield wipers sounded like sobs. Eeek. Eeek. Eeek. The woman's small blue car was parked in an alley. She was hoping to catch a glimpse of her daughter, who left work every day at around four in the afternoon.

The woman had done this before, sit in this alley and wait. She never worried about being noticed. She was sure the girl didn't even know what kind of car her mother drove these days, or anything else about her for that matter.

A few months ago, she had gone to her daughter's house and stood on the sidewalk across the street, in the dark, waiting for a glimpse. She had wanted to see if her daughter was happy, but she didn't want to embarrass herself looking the way she did. Her hair felt like straw to the touch. And no matter how much she scrubbed, the dirt was still there under her fingernails and the smell of the farm lingered.

The woman had noticed little details outside the house. There was the light turning on in a room, the shape of a black garbage bag left at the curb. Then she saw her daughter's face, framed by the kitchen window like a small photograph. She was standing at the sink doing the dishes. Her husband came into view, caressing the back of her neck before turning her around into a slow dance. Her daughter seemed happy. When you're a mother, you create a life and then you watch it go on its own way. It's what you hope for, and want, but when it happens, it happens without you.

The woman slipped back into her car and drove away.

THE WOMAN HAD WANTED to call after the stroke last year, but she didn't want her daughter to hear her slurred speech or to see that one side of her face now drooped. She didn't want her daughter to think she needed to be taken care of. She didn't want to be a burden. It had taken six months of therapy before she looked and sounded like herself again. Sometimes, when she let her guard down, like when she laughed, you could see some of her facial muscles were slow to react. Food didn't taste the same as it did before, either. Her sense of taste comes and goes now. Most of the time it all tastes bitter. And all that bitterness in her mouth is hard to swallow.

She had been working on a farm at the time. Got the job through a friend. It had been difficult to find work after the plastics factory shut down. She had been there for forty years. They don't have jobs like that anymore. The factory had paid severance, so she had a little something left over after she spent all her savings putting her daughter through school. But that wasn't the point. It was a job she wanted. Something to do for twelve hours. At least she knew how to drive. A friend had asked if she could give him and a few others a ride to the farm where they worked, and she did. She liked their affectionate teasing, the bawdy jokes they told, how they included her in all their stories, the way they took you in, no questions asked. When they told her the farm was looking for more workers, she offered to join them. "But you know how to drive and speak English better than anyone we know. You can get a job anywhere." She didn't want to tell them it wasn't true. And out of pride, she just said, "I'm bored. It'll be something to do."

It was good to be outdoors and on the land, feeling the sun on your back. She pulled weeds from the ground—the ones with thorns. She wore gloves to protect her hands, but once in a while, a thorn sharp and fine enough would pierce through. They didn't use weed killer out here, not next to the strawberries that get harvested and sold as organic. She did whatever they needed done, though—she even drove the tractor. She liked that. Seated so high above everything. But the job didn't go through the winter months, and in this country, there were so many winter months. That anything grows here at all feels like a miracle. She had to find something else to do once the cold set in.

What she found was carrots. At the farm, where the processing took place, the carrots arrived from warmer climates and sometimes came in unusual shapes. She had to discard those. No grocery store was going to buy something that looked like a balled-up fist and call it a carrot. Carrots have unique growths and bumps on their skin. No machine could handle peeling each and every one. The blades would get jammed and they'd have to shut everything down until a mechanic could come out to fix it. It was just cheaper to get somebody to peel the carrots by hand. When you work on a farm, you're just a body. You have to be there on time and do the work. Bending, kneeling, lifting, picking, pulling. And you have to do it for at least eight hours, sometimes twelve to beat the weather. You work around the weather all the time.

At first, the physical demands made her body ache—her knees and especially the bottoms of her feet. They don't hurt while you're working, when you're too busy thinking of what needs to be done and getting it done. It was at night, after a shower, when the pain would arrive.

When it happened, she didn't know she was having a stroke. She'd been tired and couldn't get out of bed for three days. It was only once she'd managed to get up to wash her face that she saw the right side of her face drooping in the mirror. When she got to the hospital, they said since she drove there herself, she was functional, and they couldn't do anything for her beyond keeping her under observation. So they sent her home. And she did go home, but the right side of her face kept sagging, and then her ear started acting up, like she was underwater. She drove herself back to the hospital, and this time they kept her for two months. How she was able to drive herself back and forth like that, she couldn't explain. But she had been lucky. When you live alone, it can take a while for someone to discover you've died. You know, the insides go first. That's what people smell when they smell a dead body. It's the insides.

ALMOST TWENTY YEARS ago now. It had rained then too. And she had been waiting in her car just like this, outside that school. Her daughter was a creature of habit. She always left the school at about four. When she had yet to appear at the doors, the woman got out of the car. She stopped the first student she saw. "I'm looking for Chantakad?" The student said, "Oh, you mean Celine?" and pointed. And there she was, standing by a locker, throwing books into her knapsack. On the inside of the locker door was a small mirror, sticky notes, magnets shaped like hearts.

When her daughter saw her mother standing there, the girl quickly slammed the locker shut and shoved at the lock. Then she ran up to her, ushered her out the door. "What are you doing *here?*" she said, urging her mother to walk faster.

"I came to pick you up," she said. "It's raining."

"*Don't* go in there again. Wait for me in the car."

"What if something happened to you? I was worried."

"Just don't, okay?"

They crossed a parking lot. The prickly cold of the rain was surprising, hitting hard at them, and there was no way to protect themselves except to run through it and get into the car as soon as possible.

"And will you stop calling me that name!" her daughter went on. "Everyone calls me Celine now." Her seat belt clicked in the back seat.

"Celine? How do you get Celine out of Chantakad?"

"That's who I am now. I'm Celine. And can you *not* talk to my friends, please? You are so embarrassing."

And how old was her daughter then—was it thirteen? Thirteen and so sure of everything. What was it about her, the woman wondered, that was so embarrassing? Was it the perm? She hadn't looked at the instructions on the package and had left the formula in for too long, so her hair now curled tight to the scalp. Was it her blue jeans, bought at the flea market and fitting high and loose like a flag around the hips? Maybe it was just that she was a mother and all mothers were embarrassing. Maybe it was just something to say to put more distance between them.

"You know," she said, turning around to face her daughter. That's what that person was back there—her daughter. But a stranger might have been more kind. "You won't understand this now, but some day, when you're a mother yourself, you'll remember what you just said to me and you'll hate yourself for having said it. You don't know what it's like to give birth, to have your body bust open like that. And then to have to clean and bathe and feed that life—just a bunch of cries and burps and shit to attend to. And I did it on my own! You just don't know!" Her daughter stared out the window as if there was something off in the distance. She went on, "But let me say this to you. And you, you remember it! You remember it! No one really wants to be a mother. But you can't know this for sure until you are one." She turned forward again, started the car, pulled the seat belt over her left shoulder and clicked it into place too, securing herself. Then she checked her side and rear-view mirrors and waited for a clearing.

EEK. EEK. EEK. There was a knock on the glass, a figure standing outside beside the car. She couldn't see who it was. For a moment, she imagined it was her daughter. But when she lowered the window, a different face appeared. A man in a police uniform. He said, "Ma'am, this is not a parking space. I'm going to have to write you a ticket if you don't move along now. You hear?"

She apologized and started the engine. It was four-fifteen and she still had not seen her daughter. Had she already passed by? Eek. Eek. Eek. It was hard to tell now what was happening inside the car and out. The blur, the wet, the rain, the sobbing.

Ewwrrkk

THE SUMMER I TURNED EIGHT, my great-grandmother showed me her boobs. Mine were just growing in, and they were sore and sensitive. They weren't large enough to fill a bra yet, but you could see them poking out from underneath my pink unicorn T-shirt. My brother's friends called them mosquito bites.

My great-grandmother lived in a house with my aunt and uncle and cousins. The two of us were alone in the kitchen; everyone else was outside, in the backyard. She always carried a basket filled with her tobacco supplies. I watched as she took out a plastic bag, reached in to retrieve a wad of dry tobacco leaves, and rolled it into a bubble gum–sized ball, which she then tucked underneath the right corner of her upper lip. Every so often she'd spit red into an empty tin can. If you didn't know what it was, you'd think she was spitting blood. The smell was as sharp as days-old urine. You always knew when she was in the room. It didn't bother me, though, and after a while I didn't even notice the smell.

She spit into her tin can, pointed at my chest, and said, "You know, you have yourself some little titties." Just like that. No being shy or subtle about it. "You should be wearing a bra." She then took off the cotton shirt she was wearing, one she had made herself. "Nothing fits this body or supports it like it used to. They don't make clothes for people like me. Think I won't live long enough to spend my money, I guess."

She dug into her home-stitched bra and pulled out her bare breasts. They looked like eggplants—not new fresh ones you buy from the supermarket, but ones that had been left in the fridge for some time.

She said, "When I was younger, all the boys liked me because of these. They all wanted to cop a feel. You'll see for yourself soon enough."

I asked her where the nipples were and she pointed to the dark lobes at the very bottom.

I thought of all the breasts I had seen up until then. My mother's were small, with large protruding nipples like pink buttons. "They used to be bigger, you know," she told me once. "You and your brother did that. Sucked all the milk out of me." And last summer, when my brother let me hang around with him and his friends, one of them stole a magazine with a picture of a naked woman on the cover from his father. Like them, I stared at her breasts.

They were magnificently large, so large they made her head seem small.

The boy did not let our eyes linger too long at the magazine. Instead, he ripped out a whole page, tore it into pieces, and sold them off one by one. A breast cost a quarter, and for both breasts you had to pay a whole dollar. He ripped out the hairy crotch for me and said I could have it for free. My brother, who was three years older than me, bought the face. It was the cheapest at only a penny. Later, we met up to put all the pieces together with some tape. They told me I had to give them the crotch shot, but I told them I had thrown it over the bridge, even though it was still neatly folded in my back pocket. I just didn't want them to have that part of her. Even so, someone put a finger into the space where the model's crotch would have been and circled it around.

"Scared?" my great-grandmother asked me now, with an amused smile.

I wasn't scared. I was amazed. "How come they don't look like the boobies in nudie magazines?" I asked.

"Don't be stupid. You think they're going to photograph or put in the movies something that looks like these? For a joke they would. But this is for real. This is what they look like if you don't wear a bra . . . well, even if you do, no matter. It all ends up looking like this." She shrugged, lifted her breasts, and stuffed each one back into her bra, patting them like flour dough. "And another thing," she added. "The first time a guy says 'I love you,' your legs will pry themselves open like this." She held up two fingers and spread them slowly to form a peace sign, and as she did this, she made the sound of a door opening on rusty hinges: "Ewwrrrkk." Then she shut her eyes tight, threw her head back, and laughed at her own crudeness. The sound of her laughter came mostly from her throat, like a dry cough.

In all the time I knew her, I loved seeing her laugh, how her face would fill with countless lines around her eyes, forehead, and dimples. When she wasn't laughing, she sometimes let me touch her face and squeeze the skin together to show the places where her laughter had been. But now her laughter wasn't something I wanted to see.

"*That* won't happen to me!" I said, shaking my head vigorously from side to side and puffing my chest out, so full of pride.

"No. Especially you. You think you're so smart, but in the end that's the thing that will get you. That 'I love you' will do it for you. It gets everybody," she said with another laugh. "Don't think you're some exception now. I know you're just a kid, but that doesn't mean you can't know things. Might not make much sense now, but it will. Eventually."

WHEN IT DID HAPPEN to me, it didn't happen like my great-grandmother said it would. It was with a man who no longer had his young face. He did not say anything that had to do with love. And, afterwards, there was a pool of blood on the grey bedsheet.

Looking at that alone, it really could have been anything.

The Gas Station

MARY BELIEVED THERE were two kinds of people in the world. There were those who were seen, and those who were not. Mary considered herself one of the latter.

She hadn't lived in the town for long, only a few months. It was known for its beaches, and during the summer it swelled with tourists, their talk and oils and heat. When it cooled, the town was quickly abandoned.

Mary was thirty-six years old. She was living in a small white house. It was one of many white houses in the neighbourhood, painted that way because of the intensity of the sun. The one she lived in had a flat roof; it wasn't a place that needed to deal with snow. Or cold. The house had one of everything. One bedroom, one bathroom, and one kitchen. Each room had a single window, which all looked out onto the same pine tree. It was not a pleasant sight.

Mary worked from home. She was an independent accountant. She didn't want to be part of anything, didn't want to answer to someone. She liked the thrill of having the whole enterprise succeed or fail with her. During the tax season she often found work by setting up a clinic or pop-up office. She had many types of clients. They all surprised her with their needs and problems and desires. Because the tax form asked you to declare a marital status, she saw every stage of love. There was the initial giddiness at having found each other, the boredom of having been together for too long, the anguish of separation, the finality of a divorce, the clinging one did in the hopes of a reconciliation that was not coming. She liked spending her days listening to people describe how things had fallen apart. It was like watching a play being acted out in front of her, the feelings raw and real—all of it up close. She didn't have to feel what they felt, but what they told her about themselves stayed with her.

Mary always remembered the last client of every tax season. The last was usually the most dramatic. The previous year, it was a woman who worked for the government. Educated, well-to-do, financially independent. She said her ex wanted to claim the child-care expenses even though she was the one who paid them. Mary reviewed the woman's papers laid out on the table and advised her that since she and her ex were no longer together, and the child lived with her, it was her right to claim the exemptions. The woman's eyes welled with tears as Mary started on the return. This went on for quite some time—Mary filling in the lines, and the woman with her tears. The woman apologized. "I've been with incredible men," she said. "Men who really loved me and cared for me. And appreciated me. But it didn't happen with them." Her story sounded like a cheap old country song. "Given my age, I didn't think I could have a baby. So when I got together with this guy, I wasn't thinking. Suddenly I'm pregnant. After all the tests, the pills, and giving up on them, he's the only one it happened with. And he was the worst!" Mary did not say anything. She continued filling out the forms.

THE GAS STATION was on the edge of town, before you hit the interstate. It was bright green, like a tennis ball. Easily spotted from miles away. This was where he worked. The gas station man. He came out to pump the gas. He was not beautiful, but she liked looking at him. Beauty was boring. To be ugly was to be particular, memorable, unforgettable even. He was uglier than that. *Grotesque* seemed right to describe him. It was not yet spring and there was a chill in the air, but the man was shirtless. He had hair like barnacles all over his chest. It reminded Mary of pubic hair, messy and wet and shining. There was something bold about him, walking around so bare like that.

From inside the car, Mary pushed the button that unlocked the door to the gas tank. She watched the man in the side mirror, where there was a note of warning that said objects in mirror were closer than they appeared.

He knew what to do each time. He came over and pushed aside the gas tank's door, reached his hand inside, and twisted the lid to a little hole. He turned, pressed a few buttons on the machine, brought over the pump, and pushed the nozzle in. Mary could hear the gasoline, how it rushed in, eager and desperate. It took a while to fill that voluminous tank.

She had seen him often like this, but they never talked. He had a reputation for being someone women fell in love with, and he was known to abandon them when that happened, leaving them wailing in the street below his window, begging to know why. Mary wondered what it was he did to make them lose themselves that way. She wanted to know if it could happen to her.

She ironed out the wrinkles on a bill with the warmth of her palms. She pressed on the side with that old man's face, and pressed again on the image of a white building on the other side. All the money in this country was green. It was easy to give away the wrong denomination. She checked all four corners for the number fifty, to be sure. He came over to the driver's side and she opened the window just a slit. The bill slid out of the window like a tongue and he grabbed an edge. Mary revved her engine and sped away.

THE TOWN DID NOT encourage much walking around. There were no sidewalks, only grassy ditches on the side of the road. Most people drove pickup trucks and at interstate speed. Every bank had a drive-through window. The tax deadline was approaching, and Mary relied on being noticed for business. It would take some time before anyone did. She had to set up her office in a public place early this year, get a head start, especially in a town like this. Besides, she could use the money. She worked out a deal with the manager of the community centre to let her set up her office there, in front of the library. She brought in a foldable desk and put out her sandwich-board sign. She thought it was the perfect place. There was a lot of foot traffic. There was a pool and a gym too.

It was inevitable, in a town this small, that she would cross paths with the gas station man. She wasn't surprised to see him at the community centre, though he appeared out of his element. His whole body was covered up. She wondered who was at the gas station now that he was here.

He noticed her sitting at her desk and came over. "Hey," he said. "Can I ask you some questions?"

She did not like how he used that first word. Hey. As though she were some hole in the wall you could just stick your questions into.

"You have to make an appointment!" she yelled. There was fury in her voice. She pulled down the hem of her skirt, which had been creeping up, showing too much of her legs—her bony ankles, the muscled curve of her calves, the rough patches of her knees, and the area above that did not tan. Her work wardrobe was two black pencil skirts, one black jacket, and two black blouses, one short-sleeved and one long-sleeved. She owned nothing else, and the clothes fit every occasion.

He looked around, then said, "There's no one here."

It was true, but she was a professional. He couldn't just walk up to her and take up her time as though it were free.

"I am a professional, sir," she said. "Professionals make appointments."

He laughed. "Okay then. Can I do that?"

While she considered her schedule, he took the seat in front of her.

"Oh. I get it," he said. "Dressed in black. Death and taxes."

She ignored his comment.

She handed him her business card and said, "How is nine o'clock tomorrow morning?"

"But I'm here now."

"That's correct, sir."

"What's the problem, then?"

"No problem. As I said, you don't have an appointment."

He seemed amused. "I never met anyone like you."

She wondered whether that statement was a compliment or not. She decided it was an observation of a fact. Well, working at the gas station, she thought to herself, how could you?

"We're done here," Mary said, making a small circle in front of her with a finger, a boundary that needed to be drawn.

He put his hands up, as if preparing for an arrest, and said, "Ma'am, I like you. Sharp. Real tough. I'll see you tomorrow." And he got up and walked away.

Mary drove home that night glad she didn't have to go by the gas station. She drove over three speed bumps on the road on purpose. She made sure she went slowly, so she could feel the rise and rise and rise and fall of the car. The buildup to the bounce was more pleasurable. Her eyes looking up at the ceiling of the car, her jaw loose and open.

When she got home, she wasn't hungry. She took a shower, washed her hair, and polished her only pair of shoes. She read a book that had belonged to her since she was a little girl. It was about a monster, but it wasn't scary at all. When she was about four, she wanted to be the beast. She roared and pounded at her chest and no one ever said that was not how a little girl should be. She could be ugly and uglier and even more ugly. She threw the book across the room. It left a dark mark on the wall, like a bruise. To be a monster, a beast of some kind. Watching everything shudder, down to the most useless blade of grass. She wanted that for herself.

THE NEXT MORNING, Mary smoothed out her black hair, dabbed some lipstick onto two fingers and patted them on her cheeks. She spread this same colour on her lips. She wore black—one of her black pencil skirts and the long-sleeved blouse.

The sky was a long, unbearable lump of grey and there was rain all over everything. It was eight-fifteen when she arrived at the community centre. Instead of making her way to the desk, she went to the bathroom. It was clean and bright with lots of room. She sat down on the counter next to the sink and pulled her skirt up to her thighs, spread her legs apart slightly, and reached in. She closed her eyes. Arched her back. Brought a finger to her mouth, her teeth clutching it there, muffling a moan of pleasure. The fluorescent lights were unflattering.

Afterwards, she sat down at her table and opened her laptop, reviewing her list of appointments. The gas station man had an ordinary name. If you searched for it in a phone book, his name would take up several columns and pages. Everyone knew at least one person who had that name.

A brown suit came into view, something definitely from

a second-hand store. The lapels were wide. It belonged in a different time and to a different person.

"I have an appointment," he said.

"Take a seat." Mary rested her elbows on the desk and straightened her back. Most people stared at a detail of her face or at the wall behind her. The gas station man took in all of her.

Then it was over and he was gone.

Mary stepped out into the rain and tried to look for something familiar to steady herself. Something had unravelled. Everything was wet and muggy. She stepped back underneath the awning, where it did not rain, and noticed a little mound of dirt. At the centre of that mound was a hole—an entrance and an exit. She imagined the networks beneath her feet. How they went on forever. She hated that it was closed off to her—the ants and their secret world of working together and lifting things greater than themselves. None of them were like her, working alone. She lifted a foot and wiped away the mound. As if nothing had ever been there. They would build it back eventually. That was the magic they had, together.

WHEN MARY GOT to his apartment building, she pressed the button in the elevator to go up to the fifth floor. It did not move at the speed she liked. It crept up too slowly, rising in jitters and jitters and then jolts. She could have walked up the stairs. It would have been faster.

Mary didn't know why she was there, only that she wanted to be.

When the elevator arrived, there was a ding, like a service bell on a desk. Her black shoes clicked on the floor and when they stopped, the door to his apartment opened. He served dinner. He explained everything to her. How it would all unfold. He said it was going to be sweet and tender and loving. Then he'd tell her he didn't love her. "It'll be a lie," he said. "I don't like feelings."

When the evening was over, she noticed the paintings in the apartment. He said he painted only with black. He had very large canvases leaned against the wall. They all looked the same to Mary, until she got closer. The thing about these paintings was their strokes. Each one was particular, distinctive. She angled a painting toward the light, revealing where the strokes changed, where they thickened, where they swirled, where they began and ended.

She was going to go home, but then she saw him sitting there on the bed. Waiting for her to do something. So she stayed.

FOR A TIME, he was tender and sweet and loving. When he was around, all Mary could ever see was the black at the centre of his eye. The world and its little towns fell away. What time it was, what day or hour, where the sun was in the sky or if it had been there at all, Mary never noticed. All she saw was him.

"I want to stay in," he'd say. He kept himself inside her, his body forming an appendage that grew out of her centre.

After a while, he said, "I don't love you." Mary did not say anything back. She saw now that his eyes were grey. And she was not there. She said nothing about love, asked nothing about it, or how he felt. "You're lying," she said.

He said, "Don't be ridiculous."

What was the difference between someone who lied about love and someone who didn't love you? Nothing.

That night, Mary packed her bags and left town. No one would know she had been there, that anything had happened to her in that place. But that didn't matter. She knew what she was for him. A void that would be immense.

A Far Distant Thing

THE MOULD ON THE WALLS started as little black dots near the floor. When nothing was done about them, they spread up to the ceiling. The mould looked like a field of black dandelions. That's one of the things I think of when anyone asks me about where I'm from, where I grew up.

My parents and I lived on the edge of a tree-lined street with well-manicured lawns and long, winding driveways that led up to three-storey houses—but we did not live in any of those houses. We lived in a one-bedroom basement apartment in the first building from the main street, before the road turned to take you deeper into the neighbourhood, before the trees turned green and thick. My parents slept on a thin sponge mattress on the floor of the living room. Before they left for work every morning, they folded the mattress four times like a piece of paper and put it into the shoe closet.

I had my own room. My window opened out to a parking lot where I saw only two things: the headlights or the exhaust pipe of a car.

My friend Katie lived in the same building, but her apartment had a balcony and a different view. We walked to and from school together, but I never invited Katie over. I didn't want her to see that my parents didn't have a bedroom, so I was always over at her place. Katie had two older brothers who went to high school. Her brothers played football, and they always had various girlfriends around, making out with them in the stairwell of our building or on the couch in their living room. I don't know what happened to Katie's father, I just know that he wasn't there, and I took that to mean it was something I shouldn't ask about. Her mother worked at the same factory as Dad.

Dad didn't like me going over to Katie's apartment. He said, "I don't want you going over there after school. I don't want you hanging around those boys and their girlfriends sucking on each other like that. I don't want you getting any ideas." What Dad didn't know was, I already had ideas—all the time. It's just no one was interested in doing anything with me. He thought Katie's family was a bunch of nobodies and I'd end up a nobody too if I kept spending time with them.

Dad always talked about life as if it spilled out all at once and we wouldn't have time to think or do anything about what was going to happen to us. He talked like he had to tell me everything now because we'd never see each other again. I'd roll my eyes at him, but that only made him go on. It always circled back to how different Katie and I were, and how I wouldn't get the same things she got in her life.

In spite of what he said, he did give me something Katie had. I had told him how much I liked the pink colour of the walls in Katie's bedroom. I couldn't stop talking about it. So Dad went out and bought a can of red paint and a can of white paint—the pink paint was more expensive because it was popular and because they mixed the colour for you at the store. Dad put a dollop of white into the red paint and stirred. When the paint was wet on the wall it looked pink, but when it dried it turned a dark pink, and there were smudges of red where the paint hadn't mixed well. The paint didn't cover up the mould. I didn't say anything about that. I would just look at those dark pink spots and smile to myself. I had my own room, after all, and he was trying.

DAD WORKED IN a nail polish factory. He had started out cleaning the floors. While he cleaned, he stood behind the workers on the line and watched them peel labels and stick them onto the nail polish bottles. It didn't seem very difficult, he said. When the factory made cuts and offered the remaining workers less pay, many quit. Suddenly there were job openings on the line, and so

Dad applied for one and got it. He got Mom a job there too. Even though those who worked on the line were now paid less than before, it was still more pay than what Dad had made as a cleaner. They both loved the job. The hours were long, but the work was steady and they had their weekends free.

One time, during his break, he told me that a man who worked on the line with him said something about the way he worked, mimicking his speed, scooping up everything around him. Dad thought it was a compliment so he pretended to pick things up too, agreeing that was the best way to work. He was happy someone at the factory was talking to him instead of pulling at the skin on the side of their eyes and laughing as he walked by.

It wasn't until the foreman laid off a few more workers who couldn't keep pace that they started to come up to him and say a word to his face that sounded like spitting. It took so much air to make that word, but the spit never arrived.

He asked me what they were calling him at the factory. "This *thief* thing. What is it?" I didn't want to tell him. I wanted him to go on liking his job, to get up in the morning with a sense of purpose and pride like he did. I told him I had never heard of this word before. Then I turned away so I wouldn't have to look at his face as he told me, "All you have to do is work hard. That's all it is, hard work."

RIGHT AFTER GETTING HOME from school, Katie and I would spend three or four hours on the phone with each other. With the sound of our families distant in the background, we talked about everything and nothing. We wanted to be writers then, and we liked to see how well we could describe the details of our day to one another, even though we were in every class together. We talked about the pretty girls in class—what they wore, how they styled their hair, how they laughed. And if one of them talked to us, we would go over every word they said, pick out exactly where the stress and silence and giggles fell, as if we were breaking some kind of secret code.

Eventually, our talk would turn to wondering what it would be like to be rich. We knew what rich people were like. We'd see them in the mornings on garbage day, coming out of their homes and carrying their garbage bins to the curb. We couldn't believe they had their own bin and could walk to their own curb. We had to carry our garbage to a tiny closet at the end of the hallway and drop the plastic bags down a hole in the wall. Katie and I were afraid someone would come up behind us and push us down the hole too. Sometimes, before taking out the garbage, we would call each other on the phone just to let the other know. "If I go missing, you know what happened," she'd say. Sometimes we would even go to the garbage chute together. For a laugh, we'd take turns pushing each other from behind toward the hole—but not too hard. Just enough for us to feel our fear and then let it go.

ON THE SECOND FLOOR of our building lived a man who didn't have a job. He sat by the window all day and smoked. When he saw me and Katie coming home from school, he'd yell out, "Hey girls. Sexsssy," and then he'd laugh like it was just a joke. He laughed even louder when he saw how frightened I was. Later, he dropped the "Hey girls" part and simply said, "Sexsssy." I hated seeing the orange dot glowing in the window above us.

Katie knew how scared I was of him. She told me to ignore him, but I wasn't like her, and I couldn't do it. "Don't worry," she said. "I'll take care of him." I didn't want her to do anything. He was an adult man. He was stronger than the both of us.

The next afternoon, when we got to the building and we heard him say, "Sexy," she looked up at him and yelled, "We're TWELVE! You creepy fuck!" And because she'd said something, I felt I had to say something too. So I shouted, "I'll cut *it* off! We'll see what's sexy then!" and we quickly ran inside the building and laughed maniacally in the stairwell. I liked the sound of our laughter then. Even though it was just the two of us there, the way it echoed and multiplied made us sound like more.

THE SCHOOL WE WENT TO was a forty-five-minute walk from our building. We rarely took the bus, except when it was terribly cold outside, but even then, we would try to walk if neither of us could manage to get the fifty cents for the fare, which was most times. Asking for fifty cents was like asking for a million dollars—when you don't have it, you just don't have it. Once, though, to teach me some kind of lesson when I asked for bus fare, Dad said, "You know how hard it is to make fifty cents? Why don't you go outside and try to find one cent." So I did. I went outside and searched the ground for some change but found none. When I came back inside, I didn't say a word. I couldn't even find one cent, so I understood how hard it was for him to make fifty of them. And yet, as I went to bed that night, I felt a coldness underneath my pillow. It was two shiny quarters.

THERE WAS A CHAIN-LINK FENCE in the back alley of the building we lived in, and behind that fence was a dense green forest. It's what separated our building from all those nice houses farther down the street. There was a small creek running through the middle of it, and from Katie's balcony it looked like the side-part in a head of dark hair. We would grab at the metal fence and pull ourselves closer and closer to the top to get to the other side. Then we would find an area to lie on the grass and describe to each other what we could see. We went there to waste time and to avoid our usual path home.

One day, when we were in the forest, Katie told me the police had found a dead body back there. A girl about our age.

"You ever see a dead body before?" she asked me.

I thought of my grandmother at her funeral. She looked so peaceful it was like she was only sleeping. When I told Katie that, she said, "Yeah, that's when it's natural."

Then Katie lay down on the ground, spreading out her arms and legs into the shape of a starfish. Her face went blank and she stared up at the sky. She lay there for about ten minutes, not moving or saying anything. In the shade, her skin appeared blue, and her collarbone stuck out. I didn't like the quiet, or feeling like I was alone in the forest. The trees hovering over me seemed human, and I could almost feel their branches reaching out for me.

"Katie! Stop it!" I yelled. "Get up!"

She didn't move.

I kicked her leg.

She started laughing. Small, soft chuckles like someone was tickling her. And then she let out a loud scream. She continued to scream and scream, blotches of red covering her face, and then I began to scream with her. We muffled our giggles in between. We knew our screaming was just a joke because we were doing it together, but I tried to imagine what someone hearing us would think.

"Scared you, didn't I," she said when we finally stopped.

"Why'd you go and do that for?"

"Just to see what you'd do. See how no one comes when they hear you screaming? You're on your own." She sounded a lot like Dad when he was giving me advice about how life was.

She went on: "Someone dumped that girl's body here. You know, it could have been me. I saw a picture of her in the paper." Then she sat up and brushed off the leaves from her clothes. She laughed again and said, "C'mon, it's getting dark."

We headed back to our building, but then Katie stopped and told me to stand still. She removed the straps of her red knapsack from her shoulders, unzipped a pocket, and reached inside. She handed a heavy grey book to me.

It was a dictionary.

I had had my eye on it all year, looking at it whenever we went to the school library. I'd thought about stealing it, but I was too afraid to ever do anything like that.

Katie said, "Look, I know you wanted this. So here"— she shoved it toward me—"take it."

I put the dictionary in my knapsack and sealed the zipper up quickly. Then, for some reason, we both ran for the metal fence as if someone was chasing and gaining in on us and we screamed like there was. When we got to where we lived, we went our separate ways without saying a word to each other.

SOON AFTER THIS, Katie and I would lose touch. Her mother got a promotion at the nail polish factory, and they moved out of the neighbourhood. Maybe it was that. Maybe it was high school. I don't think too hard on it—it was the way it was. We lose each other, or the way we know each other gets lost.

Before that, though, the last time we were together, we stood outside on her balcony to look at the sunset. We hadn't ever seen one like it before. It had something to do with the way the Earth had lined itself up in the universe. Some rare planetary alignment. The sun was large and brilliant.

I told her, "Looks close, doesn't it? Like it's someplace we could walk to and grab a piece of for ourselves."

She leaned over and clawed at the air.

I GOT TO THINKING on this time, Katie, all this stuff because I thought I saw her. I was standing at the crosswalk, on my way home after a night shift cleaning the office buildings downtown. At the sight of her on the other side of the street, and from the way she walked—assured, shoulders back, and looking straight ahead—I knew she did good with her life. She was wearing a dark blazer with a pencil skirt and carrying a briefcase. She looked the same as when I knew her, only stretched out and grown, powerful, in charge.

I wanted to run up to her, ask her if she was married or if she had kids, if she was happy. But if I asked her all that, she'd probably want to ask about me too, and I didn't want to talk about myself. I didn't want her to see me as I was in my uniform and my work shoes. Sometimes people have a way of looking at you that makes you feel you have to explain yourself.

Then I thought of Dad waiting for me at home, still in the same building Katie and her family moved out of, and I didn't want to have to explain that either. The light turned, and I watched Katie walk away from the rest of the crowd.

When I got home, Dad asked about my night at work and what I cleaned. Then he said, "Sit down, eat."

I wanted to tell him that he'd been wrong about Katie. She wasn't a nobody. Katie and I had been friends. Good friends, even. The memory of it, that it had happened, was worth something to me. I wanted to tell him that, but then he told me there was mould on the walls again and that I'd let it get out of hand.

Picking Worms

I REMEMBER THAT MORNING because I woke up to such dark. It was my mother who woke me. She came into my room and said I could help earn a little extra money now.

She'd gotten me a job with her out at the hog farm. She was dressed in dark-blue jogging clothes. She threw a matching pair at me and told me to get dressed. Then, when I was standing on the front steps, waiting for her to lock up, she handed me two soup cans with the labels peeled off. They were filled with uncooked rice. I never thought to ask what this all was for, I just went along with it, still groggy from sleep.

MY MOTHER DROVE US—it was just me and her—out to the hog farm. Driving was something she liked to do. She got her licence not long ago. She had failed the test four times, but she kept going back until she passed.

She had bought the car from our neighbour. Their daughter was going off to college, someplace far, so the girl couldn't take her car with her. It was bright orange and shaped like a jelly bean. It had tinted windows my mother didn't need. We drove out in the quiet, no radio on, the car's headlights leading us into the dark. I had the window down because I wanted the cold air to wake me.

I didn't know what kind of job my mother had signed us up for, dressed like this at one in the morning. I had heard from a friend that there are always jobs at the hog farm, for those who can handle it. You can clean the shit from the floor, or clean the hogs when they're still alive, just before they put them out on the line. Or you can rub the male ones to get them excited to mate. I didn't want that to be my job and hoped my mother hadn't signed me up for anything like that. But a job is a job, and even one like that, you could still have your dignity.

MY FIRST DAY on the job wasn't a good one. I did everything wrong. What I was asked to do didn't turn out to be so easy.

Me and my mother were the only women. There were about fifteen men, and they were all Lao like us. We were what people called us—nice. I had seen these men before at the card parties my mother went to. She cooked meals with their wives in the kitchen. When we all sat down to eat on those nights, everyone would talk about their work, their bosses, how hard it was back home, how they all came to the country we live in now—but no one cried or talked sad. They all laughed. The sadder the story, the louder the laughter. Always a competition. You'd try to one-up the person who'd come before you with an even more tragic story and a louder laugh. But no one was laughing here. Every face was serious.

Out in the field, my mother put on something like a headlamp—small, with a red light—that freed up her hands. She took out the soup cans with the rice in them and handed one to me. I followed her and tried to do what she did. To begin, she scanned the field and picked a spot far from the other workers. They talked, she said, and the sound of their talk kept their worm count low.

Then she squatted and placed the soup can on the ground near her ankle. When she moved forward, she'd also move the can so it was always within reach, shadowing her. We were supposed to wear gloves, but my mother didn't. She said you got a better grip this way. After each pick I watched her dip her hands into the soup can and rub the tips of her fingers in the uncooked rice. That was how she kept her fingers dry. She told me her hands were always cold, but she had to keep them the same temperature as the worms otherwise they could feel the heat of her hands and slip away before she got close to them.

As she crept along, she pulled worms out of the cool earth with her bare hands and dropped them into the Styrofoam cups that were attached to her lower legs with a scrunchie. Everyone had their own way of attaching the cups to themselves. Some tied them to their legs with cloth or rubber bands; others had sewn pockets onto the bottoms of their pants. Inside the cups were a few strands of fresh grass so the first pick of worms had a bit of cushion and wouldn't land so hard. It also gave the worms something familiar to feel, so they wouldn't panic and squirm around, injuring themselves. In half an hour, my mother had gone back and forth across the field four times and had already dumped eight Styrofoam cups into a large Styrofoam box, next to which was a man in charge, keeping count of her harvest.

At first, I forgot my can of uncooked rice as I moved along the line and let the slime build up on my hands, making it difficult for me to hold on to anything. I wasted time looking for the can in the field and forgot where exactly I had last picked. I didn't stay bent down and close to the earth. Every time I picked, I stood up, and by the time I got my fingers back to the ground again, all the worms were gone. They heard me coming. So I tried to stay crouched down like my mother. Even then, when I found a batch and pulled at them, they did not come out of the ground smooth and whole, but in pieces. I had pulled too hard and their bodies were broken.

The easiest way to get your numbers to be good was to find a mound of worms, all roped together and mating. When you got one of those, speed was everything, as the worms below that pile start to crawl back into the earth. But my mother got those too. She pulled at them slowly and steadily, giving the worms enough time to let go of what ground they were crawling back to and come out whole into her hand. She filled her Styrofoam cups easily, with all their bodies intact.

I didn't like how the worms felt in my hands, so cold and slimy, and raw. There was no mistaking they were alive. They never stopped slinking and slithering around, stretching their bodies out into such a length that I wasn't even sure these were worms I had just picked. I could feel their bodies pulse and throb and tickle in my hands, and they would jab at me with a head or tail—I couldn't tell which, both ends looked the same to me. I wanted to scream, to yell out about how gross it all was, and to throw them back to the ground, but I didn't want to shame my mother in front of everyone. So I held on. This was a job wanted by many, and I was lucky my mom got me in.

AS WE DROVE BACK home later that morning, still in the dark, my mother said, "That was fun, wasn't it? Picking together like that." When I didn't say anything, she added, "You didn't do so good on your first day, huh?"

I had picked only two cups compared with what was probably my mother's hundreds. It had taken so long for me to fill the cups that the worms I picked piled up and crushed my earlier pickings. I hadn't realized the weight of them would be too much. I had a bunch of dead worms no one was going to pay for. They had to be alive to be worth something.

"Next time. Next time you'll get more," my mother said. "Everyone does bad on their first day."

I thought of my father then, what he would think of us doing this, picking worms. What he would say. My father was a good man. No one who knew him had a bad thing to say about him. He died early in my life. I can hardly see his face in my mind anymore. I do remember that he used to call me Ugly. My mother said he called me that so my looks wouldn't go to my head. She said the time for thinking about looks was after you get educated and work a good job. Then looks, if they're any good, are worth something to you. But you couldn't do it the other way around.

I often wondered if my mother would marry again. Most of the people we knew were married or had someone. When I asked if she was ever lonely and sad, listening to her Elvis tapes late at night in her room, she said, "What do you want me to do? Get one of them white guys? Can you imagine. They probably will want me to say things like 'Me lope you long tie' and pump me like one of them hogs. I got my pride and I ain't lowering it for no man. I rather be alone."

YOU COULD SAY I was spoiled. I'd never had a job before, but I was fourteen, getting to be that age where it was costing my mother money to have me around. I got good grades, and so she had this idea that I might go to college someday.

Back in her country, she had never gone to school. She said a family had to have money for that, and even when there was money it went to her brothers. "Wasted it all on them, if you ask me," she said. She had seen schoolgirls in their white-collared shirts and navy-blue skirts walking to school while she sat and looked after the chickens in the yard. She was responsible for chasing all the chickens back to her property. It wasn't a hard job. It was just something her family needed done.

"I was a peasant girl. You don't know anything about that. I wanted to be wearing one of them navy-blue skirts and white-collared shirts, but I knew it wasn't going to happen for me. But it's going to happen for you. You're going to be one of them navy-blue-skirt-white-collared-wearing girls going to school. I might not have been one of them myself, but I brought someone into the world who will be. I sure can be proud of that."

I didn't tell my mother they don't wear uniforms in college here. I wanted her to have her dreams.

EVERY SATURDAY MORNING, I went back to that hog farm and picked those worms. The rest of the week, my mom went on her own and picked with the regulars. I got to be real good at it, but not like my mother. She really was a natural, if ever there was one. She didn't pick like the others. For one thing, she was the only one who took off her shoes and went barefoot. She said, "I don't like them rubber shoes. I know they can hear me coming. My feet don't make noise at all this way." Sometimes she even got to turning off her headlamp and feeling her way through the line. She knew where the worms were without having to see them, picking blind and bringing them back in large numbers. My mother called the worms "shit of the earth." She would always say, "Man, I love shit of the earth," after every pick we did.

When I got tired, she told me to take a break. I'd go sit in the car and watch her in the field. You wouldn't know just by watching them that it was worms everyone was picking. From this distance, it looked like some rich woman had lost a diamond ring and everyone had been ordered to find it. I knew my mother was out there too, although I didn't know where exactly, and I didn't worry about her as it wouldn't be too long before she emerged to hurriedly add to her worm count.

Whenever I had any time to myself, I often got to thinking of my father. You aren't supposed to remember things from when you're two, but I did. All we wanted was to live. To put it into words is to bring back what happened. He was there, his head above the water, pushing me and my mother across the river, and then I looked over and saw his head go under. He came back up once more, and his mouth opened, but he made no sound as he went under again. I couldn't swim and my mother couldn't either. But somehow she managed to steer us across, holding on to a rubber tire. Afterwards, my mother asked me if I saw what happened to my father, and I said I didn't. I didn't want her to know. Now I like to believe he ended up somewhere in Malaysia. Maybe he lost his memory and was living with a new family. Just to know he is living, that's good enough for me.

The last sound he made wasn't a sound, even.

I DIDN'T WANT to go to the school dance. But my mother insisted. She said I shouldn't miss out on things in life. I knew it was a big deal for her. She made me a pink, bubbly dress, and I tried the thing on for her to get the fit right.

Some guy at school asked if he could take me to the dance. James was his name. I thought he was all right, I guess. He sat next to me in the classes we had together. I didn't understand why. There were other seats free. He drew helicopters on the corner of my notebooks. When I asked why he went and did that for, he said, "So we can fly away together." I erased or crossed them out. When it rained outside, he would turn to me and say, "It's raining," as if it was an important thing in his life, to see that it was raining and to have someone to tell about it.

He was around me a lot because we were paired together for this parenting unit in Family Studies. I didn't want to be anyone's partner. I wanted to raise the egg we were given on my own, but James said, "I'm not going to let you raise it alone." I didn't turn him down because we got more points that way, working with someone. It was fine with me. It was just an egg, that's all it was.

When James came over to work on the assignment after school, he talked to my mother. She adored him because he looked a little like Elvis. I didn't want her to get too attached to him. I didn't want him to break her heart. I tried to get James to quit our project. I was careless with the egg and dropped it on the floor during the few hours I had alone with it. After that, I thought he'd quit on me and the project, but he said, "It was an accident. Things like that happen in life."

Still, I didn't want James to be so nice to me. I showed him my worm-picking outfit with the slime stains on it, but he didn't find that disgusting at all. He said, "That's awesome! I'd love to go do that with you sometime." I never heard of such a thing. Someone other than my mother who actually wanted to pick worms.

I wanted him to know that it wasn't awesome at all. I wanted him to see that it was hard work and you needed real skill to be a good picker. James was so good at things, I wanted to see him fail at something. I wanted to see him struggle to fill a box, to step on the worms because he didn't know where to look for them, to pull too hard and have their bodies break apart in his hands.

I wanted him to be yelled at when his count was low, and for him to depend on something for his living that he had no control of—the weather.

When I got up at one that Saturday morning, James was already having coffee with my mother in the kitchen. He wore jeans and a plain blue T-shirt. We gave him the can with the rice in it and he said, "Cool. I'm so excited!"

We drove out to the farm and he leaped out of the car. My mom told the farmer that this boy wanted to come along, that he didn't have to worry about pay because he'd work for free. The farmer liked the idea. He said, "C'mon now. Let's see what you can do."

James wore the little light on his head and started like the rest of us, but it turned out he was just like my mother. His counts were very high for a first-timer because she was the one who trained him on what to do. All the little things that had taken her months and seasons to learn and figure out on her own were given freely to him. She was there guiding him. And he picked with enthusiasm because it was her way, grabbing at those bodies as if it were all a fortune in gold.

Back in Laos, the men who worked in this field had been doctors, teachers, farmers with their own land, like my mom. None had set out for a life spent crouched down in the soft earth, groping for faceless things in the night, this shit of the earth. And they picked like it. James had never been anything else, except a kid. James picked like a man who was free.

NOT LONG AFTER THIS, James, at fourteen, became our manager. The man who owned the business said he wanted someone else to take over for him, and since James spoke English so good he could have the job. He was impressed that James had been willing to work for free the first few times. Said he was an example to all of us.

I looked over at my mother, but I couldn't see anything because it was so dark. I knew what James got was something she wished for herself. She loved this job and she had been at it for much longer than James, but no one had noticed her work at all. And James? He was happy to have a job that paid so well. He didn't wonder if he deserved the job or not. He was fourteen and he was boss.

Now my mother had some things to say about James and him getting to be boss on our drives home. It all came out then. He wasn't riding with us anymore. She said she didn't care how he got to the farm—his parents probably drove him or the farmer went to get him himself. "They help each other out like that, you know." She said, "That was nice, wasn't it? I brought that fucker, and he takes my job. What the fuck. He's a fucking kid. And they accuse us of taking their jobs. Well, you know what? That coulda been my job. My job! And he fucking took it. He doesn't even need the money. What's he going to buy with it that his parents can't get for him? I've got someone to raise. And why am I so pissed? It's just shit of the earth. Shit of the earth."

James started to change the way we picked. He said rice was something you ate, that it wasn't something to waste. The uncooked rice in our cans was replaced with sawdust. My mother got splinters drying her hands with it. The cuts got infected from the fertilizer in the soil and the sores worsened.

Then James told my mother she couldn't go barefoot anymore. She had to wear the full gear now—the rubber boots and gloves, the crinkly plastic bag with holes cut out for the head and arms. He said, "That's the equipment. You have to wear it." She did, and her harvest numbers fell.

To make up for the lower numbers, she stayed out on the field longer. She began to forget the things she once did so naturally. She didn't move with the same ease and love she had before, and the worms sensed her coming and slunk back into the ground and out of reach. I watched her heart break. She had been the best, but it hadn't mattered. The low count of her harvest now didn't tell you what had happened to the job or how it had changed. And yet the numbers could be used to say a picker was unskilled or lazy. Those things, I knew my mother was not.

THE EVENING OF THE SCHOOL dance came. Although it had only been a few weeks since James first came picking with us, it felt like a lifetime. So much had changed and become confusing to me. I knew James as boss out at the farm, and I knew James as the fourteen-year-old boy I went to school with. They seemed like different people. When I was at work, I would watch him, waiting for his newfound coldness to turn into something else, the way one waits to be loved, to be recognized as someone to be loved. I didn't look at that face too long because I didn't like what I saw, and maybe what I wanted to see had never been there.

The night of the dance, my mother laid out the pink dress I was supposed to wear on my bed. She wasn't going to be home when he came. She would be out at a card party. "I'm not going to tell you what to do, how to live your life," she said. "You go on now, if you want to go with him to that school dance. But I don't want to be here when he gets here. You know how I feel about it. I can't be nice about it all. It's just not in me. But you, you've got a chance in this life. Pick those worms and get out of this town. Be nice."

James arrived alone. He was dressed in a black tuxedo, hair slicked back, and wearing black shoes that clicked on the concrete. He had, in his hand, a pink thing that flopped. A flower.

I had turned out all the lights. It looked like no one was home. The streetlamp was like a spotlight. I could see the front lawn and when he walked into the light, I could see his whole face. It was small at first and then it got bigger, his forehead looming closer.

He rang the doorbell. Then he rang it again. When after a few minutes I still did not open the door, he started banging and struggled to turn the knob, but it was locked. He grabbed and pulled at his own hair, and it came loose and wild and undone. I saw it all, standing on the other side of the door, in the dark, watching him in the golden circle that framed the peephole. I did nothing. Not even when I heard him sob. I pressed a finger up to the peephole and held it there. I did not want him to see my open eye.

Acknowledgments

Thank you to Sarah Bowlin at Aevitas Creative Management, for your brilliance, skill, and cheer—this doesn't happen, without you. Sheila Heti. Helen Oyeyemi. Diane Williams. Madeleine Thien. Hasan Altaf. Jean Garnett at Little, Brown. Anita Chong at McClelland & Stewart, for your joy and lift and logic. Angelique Tran Van Sang at Bloomsbury. Lauren Harms, for the front cover design of this book; I love its intensity and force. Craig Young, Alyssa Persons, Ira Boudah. Jared Bland, Erin Kelly, Ruta Liormonas. Beth Follett. Kulap Vilaysack. Vinh Nguyen. Aaron Peck. Doretta Lau. Anna Ling Kaye. Bryan Thao Worra. Andy and Naomi DuBois. Andrew DuBois. Randy Travis. John Thammavongsa. Sisouvanh Thammavongsa. Phouk Thammavongsa. The Canada Council for the Arts, the Ontario Arts Council's Writers' Works in Progress and Writers' Reserve programs, and the University of Ottawa's writer-in-residence program.